To Sophia, as all my books shall be,
and to Thorn, who is very, very good.

Madness Heart Press
2006 Idlewilde Run Dr.
Austin, Texas 78744

This is a work of fiction. Names, characters, places, and incidents either are the product of the author's imagination or are used fictitiously. Any resemblance to actual persons, living or dead, events, or locales is entirely coincidental.

Copyright © 2024 Garrett Cook
Cover by Luke Spooner

All rights reserved. No part of this book may be reproduced or used in any manner without written permission of the copyright owner except for the use of quotations in a book review. For more information, address: john@madnessheart.press

First Edition
ISBN: 978-1-955745-80-2
www.madnessheart.press

KENNEL

Garrett Cook

A Madness Heart Press Publication

COMFORT

Cosmology of satin. Hitachi. Gummies. Xanax. Chocolate-covered strawberries. She may have once had a phone in here, but Cassilda had nobody in particular she wanted to reach or speak to. If she asked for one, or for clothes, she would surely receive those things, and yet she was content not to ask. Cassilda lived in a cloud of comfort, and in it, what she did was almost waiting, as she was not always sure what she was waiting for and she could take it or leave it, whatever it might be. Waiting would have been a hassle and a labor, and it was nice that she did not have that burden to bear. Life was good and she would comply, but she would be fine if nothing happened or even if nothing should happen again.

Cassilda found the wherewithal to roll, to luxuriate. She was naked; she was wanted. It felt good and it looked good to be Cassilda, curves and lips and cascade of platinum blonde hair. The bed itself moaned quietly with her as she took in these sensations, which reminded her of the contours and texture of her. The bed must have felt as nice to have her on it as she felt to be on the bed. Her body was a gift, sometimes even for her; it was nice to have and to live in such a body as hers. There was no need for doubts or for inquiries. This, this life was love and delight, where she could luxuriate and still be rich, so very rich in purpose.

Was it night now? It was dim in the room, but there were shadows. All these shadows on the wall would fade into the dark if it were night, so there was a very good chance that it was midday and the sun was high and warm outside, and it would feel nice on her skin, though it wouldn't feel so nice as the satin and the drugs and the company and the love she could feel in this bedroom where she spent her days and her nights alike. Her phone would tell her the time back when she needed her phone.

If it was night, then she should get some rest. But it might not be night, and the windows had such thick curtains that she slept just as well during the day. If she got bored, someone could bring a could bring a could bring a—*FUCK*—book. Someone could bring a book. The word was hard to reach, for some reason. It might be nice to read. Next time Trent showed up, she would ask him for a book. Yesterday, she could have asked him for a book. If that was yesterday when she saw him. It could have been that morning, or it could have been it could have been it could it could no, not that long.

She did not know when the last time she'd seen Trent was. He was handsome and put together, his cologne intoxicating, his hands so strong and so assertive. He had tied a pillowcase to her head, fucked her in the ass dry for what could have been a few hours. The gun he had thrust at the back of her head could have been loaded, but Daddy wouldn't like that, so she was probably safe from getting shot. They had cleaned up blood-slick, shit-caked sheets from right underneath her, and she hadn't noticed. Hadn't even remembered bathtime, which was a disappointment because the baths were nice and she liked the attention. She felt so alert and alive and sharp after bathtime, something to work her way down from back into the cloudy realms of comfort.

Melange of drug and cope and denial mechanism. She ate three gummies, took her pill, let her head swim, and from there, let her head swim off, down warm, substantive currents of numb, adrift from anything that could compromise this life of comfort and intoxication. She felt no trepidation, no discomfort. The doubts floated, but in their wake, she was left instead with a hunger for people, for something to resurrect that which hovered on the brink of bedbound nowhere. From the corner of her eye, she saw something stretch across the wall. It could have been the drugs, but it probably wasn't. Maybe it wasn't. She hoped it wasn't. If she could see him, he was there.

A shadow, long as her days of anticipation, stretched its way across the wall. It was tall, ceiling high, and needing to hunch over, its fingers long and slender, branches of an ancient dead tree seeking a window pane to skritch against, choosing instead Cassilda. Daddy's sharp fingertip grazed her throat, ran down, reached the space between her breasts, made circles on her belly before the sensation faded. The tall shadow was gone, the fingers retracting into nothing, the feeling of ravenous eyes gone suddenly as it had come. Strange as it was, she immediately needed it back.

"Daddy, I need it," she mumbled in the space at the edge of sleep. Daddy could have seen fit to bring back his hands, his mouth, his weight, and his validation. If the room was dark, it was dark through lack of Daddy; if it had ever gotten cold, it would be cold through lack of Daddy. For all the feelings she could wash and waste away, the absence, the absence, the absence lingered. Had Trent mentioned Daddy was visiting? Had it perhaps come up during bathtime, which was sadly forgotten? Was it the next bathtime this afternoon? Was it this afternoon, or was it night, or even morning? She could look out the window. If there'd been a window. There wasn't a window.

"Next time I see Daddy," she said to herself, "I'll ask to be brought to a room with a window."

It would be good to look out upon the city and see the people come and go, leading lives and navigating needs she no longer had and might never have again. It would be good to know what time it was or what the weather was like. It was actually somewhat sad that she had to miss out on such things, and someone as loved and appreciated as she should experience nothing sad. It would break the hearts of those who had gone through such lengths to make her days happy and languid and comfortable.

Perhaps it would be nice even to take a walk out there. She could go to a bar or shop for some new clothes. She could check in on a friend, if she had any friends outside, which she wasn't sure of. It would be good to see the city again and walk about, and she would come back so Daddy wouldn't need to miss her; moreover, she'd miss Daddy. It would be a small thing to go out and enjoy a walk for a little bit, but this small thing would bring her tremendous joy, so if she asked, then she would certainly get it.

She, of course, would not remember to ask.

 LODGING

"Put on the ears, Pup," Lenore said in Pup's head.

Pup shook their head, as they had the last time Lenore said that and the time before that and the time before that one as well. But that time, Pup didn't mean it. The ears felt weird this time. The fishnets and the skirt and the mesh shirt looked damn good, but the ears would be a bridge too far. They closed their eyes and breathed heavy, listened for Lenore's voice again, returning to that moment. Pup needed Lenore's voice just as much as they needed a new place to sleep tonight. Lenore would say it again, and it would have been great to hear just once more.

"I said put on the fucking ears," said a sterner Lenore from the past, a Lenore a whole month gone.

Pup could feel the tiny tug on the leash, felt a hard-on stir but stop. Remembered the times when Lenore had pushed their face into her cunt, squeezed tight on the leash as the lapping began. Remembered the taste and the power surrendered, the shifting, shaking, thankful body that received the tonguing. Pup needed this association, needed to drift back and to remember and to bask in love. They could almost taste the juice in their mouth as they fixed the eye makeup that tears had nearly ruined. They could almost they could almost …

Almost was almost, even if almost had to be enough, which it wasn't. Almost still stood out of the reach of now, extending a flimsy holographic hand. It had to be enough, but it was not. Nothing that had to be enough was going to be enough. Pup couldn't do the makeup again so fought back the tears from "almost" before taking another look in the mirror. They were at least well moisturized, at least concealer did its job and buried evidence of weepy sleepless nights. For all that it was worth, Pup still looked good. Their hand hovered over the phone, considering scanning contacts yet again. There could have been someone Pup hadn't thought of. They considered it but didn't pick it up. Instead, they grabbed the ears but held them at arm's length. It had been a while.

"Put on the ears, Pup," said the Lenore in Pup's head.

Pup shook their head again, this time not in playful defiance but in grief and in anger. Lenore had a lot of fucking nerve to keep giving orders even now.

"Fuck you," Pup said, almost at a whisper, "fuck you for dying."

There was a juvenile, half done part of Pup that hoped they could make Lenore mad enough that she would say something in her defense, even though this obviously couldn't be so and could never be so again. It didn't matter, though, the need was a bigger, more transcendent thing than reality. Lenore wasn't around, wasn't alive, but still Lenore was needed. Lenore had given Pup love and guidance and hope that things would get better. Lenore took that with her.

There was a knock on the bathroom door, rousing Pup from these thoughts, these agonies. It was, of course, Christian, it being Christian's place, the last place Pup could set up and sleep and live easy.

"You okay?"

"Yeah," said Pup, opening the bathroom door, revealing that they were still just getting ready and getting psyched up.

Christian put a firm, strong hand on Pup's shoulder. It felt nice. It had been nice staying there. It had been nice hanging out with and knowing and getting fucked by Christian. Even if it wasn't the life Pup had just come out of and lost, it wouldn't have been half bad to stay here and live with a nice, handsome, professional guy who was a generally a calming influence and had a pretty nice cock to boot. Pup wanted to turn around and kiss him but didn't necessarily want to redo the lipstick, which had been tough enough with trembling, nervous hands.

Pup knew Christian loved his wife. Pup knew he loved his condo. Pup knew he loved his religious in-laws. Pup knew he loved the life he led but lived in some discomfort because he loved more things and people than it could accommodate without buckling at the knees from time to time. Pup was sympathetic to that, to a point, but had given up a lot to be able to toss aside the old name and just be Lenore's faithful Pup. Christian could have done something like it but had things to lose and to compromise and was living halfway in and halfway out of those choices. Lenore had had some words about that and how far you trust closeted allies, and yet when Pup had seen Lenore and Christian fuck, Pup had pangs of jealousy and hadn't felt those often, watching Lenore.

"I'm sorry this couldn't be a better place to stay," said Christian.

Pup could have concentrated on the death of the woman they loved, let themself become entrapped once more in the day of the text that declared the end of everything that had ever made them feel good and valued and loved and of all the freedom to be whoever they wanted to be instead of just another runaway queer kid with no connections to everyone and everywhere they'd come from. Pup could have let themself glance into the great abyss ahead where there were no friends, no home, and no comforts anywhere near as good as those they'd found here at Christian's. Pup instead saw Christian suffering, imagined how much pain they were in, thinking about their failure to do right by a dead friend. A failure to do right by Christian was similarly a failure to do right by Lenore. The two were entangled in this moment, in these anxieties.

"It's been a great place," Pup replied, stroking Christian's hand. "You've been really good to me."

"I'm glad to hear that," Christian replied, a little choked up. "Lenore mattered a lot to me. I loved Lenore, and she was always there whenever I needed her. I wish that my wife could understand the part of my life she occupied, but she's not like that. I really wish …"

"It's okay," said Pup, soft brown eyes laser focused on Christian's. "It's really okay. You smoked me up, you fed me, you gave me a place to sleep for a week. You're a decent guy."

Pup's hand instinctually went for Christian's zipper. Pup needed the conversation to be over, and this was the best way to end that conversation, at least the best one that Pup could think of and the one that Pup could count on. It was a quick blowjob, obligatory but enough to get the job done quickly and leave Christian shaking a bit and unable to focus on the maudlin parting that they didn't want to have. There was no use putting any more thought into how the situation could have been better and shouldn't have fallen apart. There were a lot of ways it could have been better, and none of them even began to play out in either of the three lives involved.

"Shit," Christian panted. "Thank you."

Pup licked their lips, forced a smile, considered a whimsical bark but knew that wasn't Christian's bag.

"My pleasure."

Christian zipped up, collected himself.

"I can give you a ride at least. Dana's plane doesn't get in until nine."

Pup nodded.

"Sure, if it's not too much trouble."

"No, Pup," said Christian, "it's no trouble at all."

Rough as the parting was going to be, Pup was grateful, clustering together and hoarding tiny bits of kindness. They had been rare and precious before, and Pup would need to keep them close to remember that survival is something they wanted, something Lenore had wanted for them. This meant playing the game. Pup barely knew how to play the game.

The ride to the club was replete with this reminder. If Pup had been any kind of hustler, they could have gotten cash for a night at a motel out of Christian, but the time for that was gone, and Pup didn't like the idea of squeezing anything more from someone Lenore had felt so close to.

"This doesn't feel safe," said Christian as they reached the nondescript red building that was blatantly clandestine in its tinted windows and obscured signage. It was easy to see that this was a place that valued discretion and maybe didn't place as much of a premium on safety.

"It's not," said Pup, "but it's what I've got right now. I tried callin' some people, but nobody had a spot, so, here we are."

"There are shelters," said Christian.

Pup replied by stepping out of the car. Fishnets.

Heels. Ears. Collar. Leash. Corset. Pup checked themself out in Christian's rearview mirror. The makeup hid the circles under their eyes with startling effect. Pup looked damn good, good enough that Pup wished they would have a chance to enjoy this. Maybe at least there would be a good fuck or two to be had out of this situation. Maybe at least a scratch behind the ears, a strong tug on the leash, a few mouthfuls of pussy, a Xanax or two. Pup turned around. That ass would make it through the night.

"Goodbye, Christian."

"I'll keep in touch," said Christian.

"Sure," said Pup, knowing Christian wouldn't keep in touch. The car pulled away, and Pup could be sure the driver would do the same. Christian and the car and the condo and the flimsy links to the outside world and Lenore's connections and a dead partner that Pup had loved more than life vanished in the distance. Knowledge of what tomorrow would look like parted from Pup's life. Pup couldn't cry and ruin the makeup.

"Be cool, Pup," said Lenore from some point where there was Lenore. "You won't fuck up 'cause you can't."

"Easy for you to say," said Pup to themself. "You're already dead."

THE BIG ROOM

Lex gargled Popov to kill the taste of smegma and ashy nicotine piss in his mouth. He was grateful that though the taste lingered, the memory of the rough fucking and sheer degradation was spotty, like most of Lex's memories had become. There were the little rooms and Daddy's friends and Daddy, and there was the big room where Lex and the others lay on second-hand mattresses and waited for the next john or, sometimes, for the next reward. There on that mattress, one of five, Lex struggled with the taste and the torment. A new black tank top, some poppers, a few rubbers, and a scalpel were sitting on it. This couldn't be his life anymore; this couldn't be anyone's life.

"I know we don't talk anymore, God," said Lex, "but I need you to take me out of here."

On the mattress beside him, Asha, scrawny, beat-up, cig-burned Asha, jumped up, mortified. Ears perked, posture declaring a readiness that would be the last thing you'd think of when you thought about Asha. A lot of things could make Asha snap, but this one made

Asha snap hard. The look on her face was pure dread and menace, holy terror that sound minds couldn't reach for in their worst moments and unsound ones had a hard time bouncing back from. Her expression went beyond "bad trip" and into implications that she knew more than she did, and in her hypersensitive junkie state, that was, in a way, sort of true.

"I heard you prayin'," she said. "He doesn't like that. The name of God burns his ears and fills his heart with wrath and thirst for revenge. You should be careful, Lex. You should consider that God's all the way up in Heaven and Daddy's right here."

Lex shook his head. He knew that Asha was speaking from a long, deep K hole and from deprivation of things that were so much more important. He knew that Asha was having trouble and almost intrinsically was having a bad time with the drugs that were keeping that fragile body going in spite of its and her desire to have done with all that she was living through.

"He's in your head, Asha," said Lex. "He's fucking with you. He's an old pervert with old pervert friends who has a gift for tricking and using anyone he feels like."

"Naw. It ain't like that. I just know better, Lex. You think this is just some warehouse space. This is his temple and his sanctum, where he is at his strongest. Daddy has power, real power, like few people in this world possess. Daddy can talk to the mean things in this world, the bats, the rats, the roaches. He chooses if he can be seen or known and whether he is the size of an ant or a giant. Don't act like you ain't seen him slip under the door or looked in the corner and saw him nearly invisible, six inches tall, watching you, or felt him get bigger, taller, stronger and that he could rip you apart inside when he fucks you. He can make rain and thunder, and there are sparks at the tip of his fingers. He is nothing like other men. Don't pretend, Lex."

Lex took another big pull of Popov.

"I'm just trying to endure this shit, Asha. I want some kind of hope."

"If you ask for hope, Daddy will give you the opposite," Asha replied. "He did not build any of this so that hope could come through. His eyes are everywhere; his ears are the mites in every mote of dust. Please be careful, Lex, I have grown to love you."

"Heat will be off," said Houston, on the mattress across from Lex's, reapplying a violet lipstick. "Daddy's gone a-hunting."

"They give you lipstick," said Lex, starting to hiss a bit. "They give you lipstick; you put it on. Un-fucking-real."

"The alternative," said Asha, grinding against the pink teddy bear on her bed, "is worse. Perhaps because it can't be known. In the end, if the end means anything, we will all find comfort in the arms of the unnatural."

Houston was looking good, ass and hips and breasts blossoming more, implying a fecundity that could hardly thrive under conditions such as these. Lex wanted to be happy for and supportive of Houston, who was taking medicine instead of just drugs, but there was something real fucked-up about how she lived in this space and how she was starting to think about life here. Cassilda had been brought up, and Cassilda had been eager to do so. It was weird that there was a straight girl with them, but Lex had grown to love and appreciate her, and Luna had an amazing time using her as a personal Barbie doll, making her up, primping and prepping her for what she always wanted to pretend wasn't survival. Fucking Luna. Fucking Cassilda. Fucking Houston.

Luna's eyes shot open, thanks to the volume of the

conversation. Luna slept a lot, not as much as Cassilda did, but still, Luna would rather be sleeping than awake most of the time. Luna had let herself go on the fast food and the edibles and the lack of exercise, and was seen less and less. She had been a voice of reason, empathy, and patience while she was conscious, but there was less of that than before. Things were changing here.

"Stop being a dick, Lex," said Luna. "This place sucks enough without your attitude. Somebody could come and this could all be over, but not if we just let it take us away."

"Gus isn't coming back," said Asha. "Cassilda neither. These things are not disconnected."

"Maybe," said Houston, "I want to feel pretty, and maybe I can't afford my pills out there. Maybe I don't just want to break down and die in this basement. I think it doesn't have to end like that."

"We're going to die in this basement," said Asha. "Not much else to be done. But you don't have to be scared. It'll be nice and dark and quiet when we die. Like my head is right now."

Lex reached out to the moments before the big room in the basement, looked around for what he was, what he expected, where he liked to eat and drink and walk around. Lex tried to remember what there was beyond his thirst and urges and fears. He knew there had been a time when he prayed and he expected that which he prayed for to come to pass. He knew that. And he knew there was a lot missing. He did not know where he'd learned to pray and who had taught him.

He couldn't figure what had been there, couldn't even imagine it. Maybe he was just going crazy, as anyone could and should in this place, as everyone could and should there. Maybe his mind had been fragile out there and had decayed and faded, or maybe someone or something had gone and reached in there and yanked out all that he knew out there. Maybe this was new to him, or maybe this was something he did and felt every day here, however many days that had been.

How many days had it been? How many of these people had he gotten to know and grown to care about and been shuffled on out? Lex could not find these answers, though there were names and there were experiences and there were voids where they had been but no specific answers. He looked into the dilated brown vortex of Asha's eyes and saw the final flickers of a person burning out as fast as he.

"I'm sorry," said Lex. "I'm sorry I was a total dick. I love you all."

Houston came to him, held him tight, pressed his head to her chest.

"I will tell him that he needs to let you go. He loves me, and he knows that I love you. He knows that I want you all to be safe and happy, and he is going to do it. We're not going to lose anybody else; I promise."

Lex let himself be cradled. Lex let himself feel the tenderness, the kindness, the patience, and the optimism that had made Houston who she was, even in the wake of the horrible things they had endured. He listened to Houston over Asha, though Asha, in her way, really knew the score. He wanted them all to be safe and free and maybe, out there, if there was an out there for them, to build something new and beautiful in their lives, something completely unlike the hell they were living.

"I know you think that, I know you need what he gives you, but maybe—"

"It doesn't seem like it, Lex, but I swear to you," said Houston, "this is a good place and it's going to keep getting better for us. We don't have to be afraid like Asha says. He's powerful, but his power is loving. He is so beautiful, you know that. If he wasn't good to us, I wouldn't love him, and I love him so, so very much."

Lex wanted to shake her, slap her, wake her from the trance she was walking around in, break the veil of bullshit, but when he searched himself, he could not find the words. Words like captive, words like slave, words like torture, words like rape faded from his mind when he tried to say them and even when he tried to think them. He knew that he could not get out and they could not get out and that he wanted some God that he had spoken to somewhere and sometime in his life to free him, but beyond that, those thoughts left him as quickly as they had entered his mind. He spoke up, and the words that came out were fully of his choosing, fully the truth as he knew it, even if they were not the ones he was initially choosing.

"I love him too, Houston. I love Daddy so much."

THE CLUB

Pup closed their eyes and let the Lenore inside their head in, let her speak and think and live beyond the grave—the only place she could—and there, she lived with an acuity unmatched by any of the other dead folk in Pup's life, an acuity Pup never stopped and questioned because it seemed so natural. Pup needed her desperately in order to think the way Lenore thought, to approach this as Lenore had approached it before. They had gone to a place like this in Alexandria, Virginia, and another couple like this one in town, though more savory. The bathhouse would have been a better night, but there were no events at the bathhouse, so the traffic wouldn't be what they needed. Too casual too. Pup needed to match the bit of desperation.

"So, you gotta remember," said the Lenore in Pup's head, "that these places cater to a few different kinds of clientele. You get nervous voyeurs. They might head into the theater or they might get too scared and stay in the hallway. You get couples looking to find a little spice and excitement. You get presumptuous Doms, and you get dangerous pervs. You have to know one from the other."

In spite of simply speaking to a model of a person, Pup found themself listening acutely, nodding along to the phantom words from nonexistent lips in order to seek out some manner of safety and security, to extract a night of life from a potentially dangerous place. Maybe, if Pup played their cards right, even a few nights.

Pup walked into the club, let in by an apathetic dude in a utilikilt who seemed like he'd rather be literally anywhere else. Pup walked past a series of gloryhole booths, deciding that they were not the place to make a connection that lasted more than about ten minutes. The theater space further in the back might have been better, but the playrooms would be a lot more promising. Pup had been to places like this, where Lenore had found friends and clients to help keep things going. Hadn't made it out to this one and didn't remember much about what Lenore had to say about the place.

It sounded like the place was virtually dead. Pup could have left and found someplace else, but there didn't seem to be real events at any of the clubs or bathhouses in town. Pup was not rolling in options and wouldn't do great on the street or stroll. Lenore's old advice played over again and only rang truer. Pup watched a few shy young guys mincing around indecisively before one disappeared into the gloryhole booth. The other took his eyes off his shoes and moved them to the exit. Must have decided this wasn't the night for whatever. That didn't bode well.

An older guy with a heavy paunch and his wife, who looked like she taught eighth grade social studies in Wisconsin, caught Pup's eye, and Pup caught theirs. Nothing much needed to be said before the three disappeared into a private room. The wife found a corner and put her hand down her jeans as her husband made himself comfortable, then beckoned Pup onto his lap, where Pup quickly sat down, throwing in a theatrical wiggle for the benefit of the masturbating voyeur wife in the corner. Hopefully, a good performance in this nigh empty fuckvoid that had no features, save the stuffed chair and a stool the wife could use but was choosing not to, would earn them a place to stay.

The man toyed with Pup's pink hair, rubbed Pup's fishnetted legs. A shudder went through the man and his excited wife as he began to suck and nibble gently on Pup's throat just above the collar. It was awkward, stubbly, and more than a tiny bit performative, but Pup felt wanted, Pup felt a tinge of purpose and acceptance, a desire to make these two happy that they chose to go out to this club and express something they didn't get to. Pup was grateful to have that, grateful to be a source of joy and pleasure, though they came so hard to Pup in light of the loss.

Pup shifted, wiggled, lap-danced, worked the scene, and tried to get the guy hard enough to fuck. It was tough knowing that a chance at staying off the street was contingent on a guy their dad's age getting hard in public, but it was probably the case. The intimacy, connection, and loyalty could tug the heart strings and libido all at once. The wife was having a great time; the husband was having fun, but things weren't escalating, so Pup whispered in the guy's ear.

"You want a blowjob, baby? It would be really nice to suck your dick."

The man shook his head.

"This is good; I like this."

Pup didn't want to push too hard. These people were happy with this, even if it wouldn't become what Pup needed. Pup wanted this man and his wife to be happy and wanted them to feel that someone was there to make their life better, like the beloved pet that had made a cruel childhood with people that didn't understand them easier. Pup was Pup, and to be Pup was to be a loving, compliant, gentle, and optimistic creature, even when the actual cruelty and madness of life got in the way. Pup got a stir from this man who had probably held back this part of his life a lot in the past and not known what to make of himself in an outside world that was nothing like this nice, private room for the three of them.

Nobody was particularly spent by the end of it, but everyone was more or less done. Pup liked the feel of skin, the moan of approval, the knowledge that they were desired by everyone in that room. Pup floated on it, even if it didn't fix the main problem Pup was hoping to. As the three made their way into the hallway and scattered, parting ways, Pup was not governed by deflation or disappointment but, for whatever it mattered, instead recharged and reaffirmed of all that they had to offer. Pup could make people feel good, and that mattered, no matter what the night and life had taken away.

There was a guy wandering back and forth, dodging the eyes of anyone. He was a longshot, but maybe he'd seen something or someone of interest.

"Hey," said Pup to the twitchy guy, "I'm trying to find a place for the night."

The twitchy guy looked Pup over, rolled over some thoughts, then dismissed them.

"I don't think I can put you up."

"Okay, cool," said Pup, turning around to head toward the theater after meeting what seemed like a dead end.

"Wait!" said the twitchy guy. "I think, yeah. Wait."

Pup nodded and waited.

"Daddy, you gotta talk to Daddy," said the twitchy guy. "You're totally his type."

"You gotta be more specific," said Pup. "Half the guys here wanna be called Daddy."

"Yeah," said the twitchy guy, reaching into his pocket and passing Pup a THC gummy, "but Daddy's Daddy. Balding guy, dressed Goth, funny looking but kinda fabulous. Legend around here."

Pup ate the gummy without reservation, then turned toward the crowd heading to and out of the club's many private playrooms. Some of these people would be big shots, and some were shy couples, but this would be the place to find a dude calling himself Daddy, or at least one of those many dudes calling themselves Daddy. Based on what the twitchy guy had said, it didn't take long to narrow it down to one very obvious prospect.

Indeed, he could be called underwhelming. The red velvet goth was 5'11" upright, but slouch and paunch brought him down to Pup's height, though a three-inch top hat corrected for the slouch somewhat. His hair was a steel grey, long and stringy, and the small mustache he wore suited him, even if the whole ensemble reeked of try-hard and poser. And yet somehow, as Pup approached, nerves were starting to kick in.

"Excuse me," said Pup to the red velvet goth, "I heard you were a lot of fun to play with."

"Yes," said the red velvet goth, "I do have a reputation for showing subs a good time. Are you a sub looking for a good time, then?"

"I'm a sub looking to give you a good time. I go by Pup," said Pup with a forced smile.

The guy took Pup's hand and kissed it.

"Enchantez. Le Comte, some call me. Though I'm more commonly known as Daddy around here."

Pup smiled.

"You know half the guys here go by Daddy."

Daddy laughed; it was big and theatrical. It was too much, but there was something charming in how histrionic it was. It made him seem less like a predator and more like a character. While the two often intersected, Pup felt safe in this guy's company immediately. He was goofy, but he was probably harmless. Probably harmless was good enough. Probably harmless was a hell of a lot safer than a lot of people at the club.

"I assure you, if you ask where to find Daddy, you will be directed to me. I suspect you might already have been."

"Wanna show me why they call you that?"

Daddy gave Pup's leash a tug, drew Pup close, let them melt into an intense kiss. Daddy's breath was better than it seemed it would be; his kiss was eerily sweet; a tiny nibble on Pup's lip drew a little drop of blood. Pup was not much for pain, but this, this was a different. Pup leaned into this, let it fill them. Bite more bite more, but there was no second bite coming. Pup couldn't speak to beg but could tell that even had they done so, Daddy would hold back. Daddy would be about the precipice of anticipation; Daddy would be about making Pup beg.

Daddy was about easing Pup to their knees, fishing out a reasonable, not altogether ostentatious tool, and then shifting from that sensual kiss and bite to transition into a skull-fuck that left Pup gagging but eager to keep up. Pup looked up, met Daddy's eyes, and got lost in them in a way that they were not expecting. There was something too beautiful for words in there, something so beautiful that Pup felt like crying—for the first time since Lenore, not for Lenore or for themself but for the wealth of beauty and bounty and possibility, for the dark and exciting and dangerous, as well as for the tender and the warm and the loving. Pup's eyes and mouth watered in unison as Daddy reached into his coat and took out the lube, reaching up Pup's skirt to start to spread it.

"Are you going to be my good doggie, or you gonna be a bad doggie?" Daddy asked.

As Daddy spake the words, there came into being, like through the work of Old Testament God, a category of creature called Bad Doggie. And the category brought with it a powerful dread that Pup could become a Bad Doggie somehow. Pup was not reluctant to get fucked, but Pup was now very afraid that there could be such a thing as Bad Doggie and that that could be Pup.

Daddy pulled his cock from Pup's mouth so that Pup might answer, and Pup knew that it would be important and that it would be terrible, unthinkable even, to disappoint Daddy in any way. Daddy then got up behind Pup and worked his way inside.

Pup shuddered as the throbbing cockhead made its way in. He gave Pup just enough time to acclimate to a cock inside before thrusting deeper. The grip on Pup's hips was iron, a bit imposing but still secure. With Lenore gone, Pup had never felt "somebody's got me." They had felt that Christian cared and Christian would do his best but could not find it inside themself to think they were being held on to securely, that they were connected. In this conduit of bodies, Pup was connected, this link from head to tail to heart to head to heart Pup let themself into. It was too good and too pure for this place, but Pup ignored that, choosing instead just to feel it, choosing instead that the way to live was to live this and let it be and let it make life right.

"Feels good, right?" said Daddy.

"Ruff," said Pup.

"I've got you," said Daddy. "I've got you."

Daddy scratched Pup's hair. They swore they could feel a tiny tingle of static, a gentle pinprick of heat and shock. Pup pushed back onto Daddy's cock, which throbbed and reshaped around the body that welcomed it, gripped it, embraced it. Something was between them, something Pup couldn't see looking at the fairly nondescript and schlubby stranger. Pup had cum, hard at that, but Daddy was still going, playing this body as an instrument of pleasure, driving in an uncanny rhythm, thrill of servitude, triumphal fuckfog. Pup had done no poppers and yet could go on forever without getting sore; this strength could bind and bend and break, but that didn't matter.

There was no thought of "this is weird" or "this is sudden," no admonishment from the Lenore inside, no thought there should be a Lenore. Pup could search their mind and soul in this moment and would not find anywhere, no matter how deep or thorough the search, a trace of doubt. Daddy's fingernail in Pup's side dug deep, deep enough that it drew blood, and it should have been a thing that made Pup want to wiggle away, but it was instead another kind of being had, a scrape of flesh, a drop of fluid from one who could be trusted with custody of this body.

"You're coming home with me, Little Dog," said Daddy.

Pup barked in assent.

BRIDAL SHOWER

"Daddy, is that you?" Cassilda asked the sound of movement even before a person coming in was attached to it. It, of course, wasn't Daddy because when Daddy walked into a room, she could never hear it.

"No, Baby," said the man who walked in first, "you know who it is."

The man's hair was wild; his eyes screamed "meth." His cock was out already, and he was working it. He was accompanied by four other guys, old but muscled, old but clearly able to fuck her up if she did not comply. There was no need to worry about that, though, this was Cassilda, who couldn't remember the last time she uttered the word "no," nor would she really wish to. Declining things was not Cassilda's way nor had ever been. Cassilda did not get where she had gotten by saying "no" to anything.

There was love to be found in that weathered face because Daddy had bade her to find and take in that love. She wanted Daddy, but she took in what she got, juicy, thirsty, and inviting, slipping him in deep as the guy's cock could manage. Daddy was bigger, Daddy felt better, but Daddy wanted this, and to do for Daddy was to show Daddy's very good friend the love that he deserved. And Daddy's next very good friend. And then two others. A blur of bodies. A blur of use.

Were they hurting her? Some were slapping; some were choking. One was holding her nose as he fucked her face, her lungs refusing to take in air. Teeth on her nipples, tugging rough. A finger in her ass by complete and unasked for surprise. They might have been hurting her. Daddy? Daddy would have known if this was hurting. She could not know on her own what was pain and what was loving, as that was Daddy's choice, not hers. This was very nice, and she had the drugs and the treats and the love that she wanted. These men worked hard for Daddy, and they deserved to feel good. Cassilda liked to feel good and to share those feelings with others.

She did not know how long they went before the last of them pulled out, exhausted. She knew her legs were feeling fine. She did not feel raw or hurt or like her legs were going numb. Daddy would not allow her to feel bad like that. When they were gone, she missed them, since now she was alone and once again hungry for touch. She reached for the pills. She reached for the Hitachi wand. She contemplated the emptiness of her cunt and what could and should have been in there. Daddy should have been in there. Daddy did what he could, she knew that, but what she wanted most from Daddy was simple: what she wanted was more.

She was not alone for long. Three of the men walked in the room holding a young lady by her arms. She was not struggling. A garland of violets, sewn haphazard by talentless hands, sat upon her head. She smiled beatifically, befitting a young woman adorned in white gown and floral garland. She could have stepped out of a Renaissance painting looking like this, but she was here waiting for whatever these men were to do.

She was very attractive. Maybe they'd want her to sit on Cassilda's face. Sometimes, Cassilda got pussy. Sometimes, Cassilda entertained Daddy's wives. That was nice. She liked the smell and the taste of them. She might like the smell and taste of this woman.

She was surprised to see Trent walk in. Trent was carrying a knife. Sometimes, Trent carried a knife. The woman was bouncing in place with excitement, with anticipation. Sometimes, Trent liked to cut Cassilda and taste it, and that was fine. Trent was forceful and powerful like Daddy. She liked that about Trent. Maybe Trent would have a shot next, fucking her while this woman sat on her face. Fuck. That would be nice. The taste of cunt and the pounding of an angry and passionate cock while these men watched. FUUUCK. Cassilda was getting wetter; Cassilda was shuddering with anticipation. What was coming next?

Trent revealed what was coming next with a single unceremonious flick. He let a rare smile cross his face as he looked at Cassilda and slashed this woman's throat. A fourth man held up a bucket, taking in the blood from the cut in her throat and gathering it, his eyes full of hunger and sadism, like those of Trent. With a second stroke of the knife, he sliced open dress and right breast alike, another wound for the blood bucket to gather. The woman did not shriek, did not twitch, did not resist in any way; she simply stood and awaited more of Trent's knife.

In her mind, Cassilda was shrieking out the words "Stop! You can't do this!" but her face and body showed awe and perhaps arousal, mouth opened into an impressed and impassioned "ooh!" beckoning the crew to thrust the knife in yet another time, another and then another. A splash, a spray, a burst of blood into the bucket. In the arms of the crew, the young woman thrashed and gave herself to the knife, then they ripped it out and gave more of her to the bucket.

What was it? Why drained and wasted? Why reduced to spray and splash and squish of fluids, a woman standing there waiting to die? She had to ask the questions and make them see and make them stop, but it was oh so nice to be wanted and afloat on drugs and hormones and the approval of that singular shadowy master of her life. Why should she ask? Was it wrong to kill? Someone seemed to have said a thing to that effect at some point, but she looked so good all wet and shiny and her face all full of the light that was about to leave, a personlight extinguished with loving and sacred and ceremonial care for ends that could only be in the very best interest of her and everyone else she had known.

Cassilda watched, confused, still jarred as they took the bucket and brought it over to her.

"Stand up straight," said Trent. "This is for Daddy, you see."

"For Daddy?" said Cassilda drowsily as she got to her feet and approached Trent.

"Yes," said Trent, holding up the bucket, then dumping its contents in their entirety onto Cassilda.

Cassilda was at first nauseated, at first repulsed, at first feeling like she should run and tell someone, someone who she could tell, Daddy, yeah, she'd ... but then it was exuberant, then it was the raw unbridled life that she expected to find, that bucket, the life that had been torn and drained out by the thirsty blade and Daddy's thirsty friends, and it was hers now, it was enough to shock her mind awake, enough to clear away the drugs and clear her eyes. She wanted to show her objection to them, to tell them she now understood what they were doing, that she was sharp now and strong now, and they couldn't possibly, no never no never no never get away with this. She could do something or find someone to do something about this. She reached out, covered in blood and full of rage, and her hand instinctually shot out to seize Trent's throat.

"Yes," said Trent, "that's it, go on."

Trent's hand was wandering toward his zipper as she started to squeeze, staring into him, trying to know why it was that he had decided to do this to her even though it felt it felt it felt it felt kind of nice. She felt life and breath fleeing from him, waxing, then waning but supporting and giving life to his hard-on. He wasn't suffering under her touch; she wasn't avenging anything. The rage was turning Trent on. Cassilda let go, surprised to find herself letting out a feline yowl.

"We will go," said Trent, gathering his breath. "We will use this thing, this generous doll, until her insides come apart. Then we'll dispose of it."

"You killed her!"

"To move things along," said Trent, turning and taking his leave, dragging the young woman's corpse like a little kid would a cherished stuffed animal.

There was something wrong with this, something wrong with him. Everything was so confusing, and the world had a vivid new focus. She wanted more from it, maybe everything. Yes, everything was to be tasted but not as it had to be before. Before she had been fed; now she felt she wanted to hunt. She let them go out of courtesy for Daddy, though something in her, a nascent growl, didn't want her to.

She was drenched in a dead woman's essence; she was feeling something so unlike what she felt before. She could be mad and sad and bothered if she chose, and Daddy let her. There were limits still to what she could think and feel but there were so much fewer than there had been before; there were complex and unwelcome thoughts, memories even of a boyfriend she had ditched, of a family she didn't call, of a friend of a friend who had known a place back in this old life where she had been something besides an intoxicated and exploited object of adoration. There were friends down in the big room she didn't see and friends outside she'd never see. She felt now that if not for Daddy, she would choose to leave. In the blood, some of her that was lost was found again.

"Daddy!" she screamed out to the only one who could and would bring clarity to her racing, stuttering, transforming mind. If Daddy knew what had gone on here, Daddy would be furious at those who'd done it and never let them get away with killing this girl and then splashing her with warm, delicious blood. She licked her lips, wiped some from the side of her face. It was nice, the blood, but how they had gotten it wasn't. They needed to be held accountable. She lapped her fingers clean of blood, then wiped off another dollop and sucked it from her mouth, letting out a contented "oooooh."

If the men came back, she would fall upon them and rip and shred, and in them, she would take blood for the blood for the blood they took. It was only right. These men were killers and could not be permitted to kill again. That woman had people who loved her, a family perhaps, and they, they had so very much blood and life in them and she could fall upon them, and with zeal and cruelty, she could make it hers. It would only be fair. Daddy would need to bring them, though, and he would because these men had done her wrong many, many times and they would have to pay.

"Daddy!" she called out again, feeling that he was closer than ever and had been watching and listening and taking it all in, and surely Daddy, wise and caring Daddy would know well enough how to fix this.

"I am here," said Daddy's voice from every corner of the room until he appeared before her, growing to his full glorious and imposing height.

He stood so tall, his body hunched at the ceiling, bent, elongated, impossible. She looked up in awe, clapped like an infant, and then fell to her knees as towering Daddy looked down, arms and legs bent into unworkable angles that suggested perhaps that he had unburdened himself of bones. Daddy was as large or as small as he chose, as kind or as cruel as he chose, but was always Daddy and always deserved all her love.

Cassilda crawled to him, held out her arms, and clung to those impossible stilted legs, needing him to make it clear and clean and easy again and forever. Daddy could do that. Daddy would do that for her because she was precious and special and loved by all.

"Daddy, they killed her. I don't know who she was, but they are killing people here, and I … I look like this."

The long fingers ran gently up and down her shoulders, caressing and rubbing that long ago spilled blood into her skin. She trembled under them; she sighed at his touch and let the sticky redness start to sink into her deep as it could. Daddy gave a whispered shush as he stroked and massaged her, and she in turn did hush as if those nails had scraped away a layer of questions that barnacled her skin.

"They kill because they love you, they want you to thrive and stay beautiful for all of your days, days that will be so much longer than you could have ever dreamed. Do you trust me?"

"Yes, Daddy. You treat me so good, Daddy, and I know you would never hurt me in a thousand years."

Daddy seemed to shrink until their eyes met.

"Yes, Cassilda, not for a thousand years."

"Nobody, nobody has loved me like you. All I want—"

"I know everything you want," said Daddy, strong hands upon her and bringing her down to the mattress.

Daddy's cock. She was getting Daddy's cock. It was rare to know she could get it anytime she wanted, she wanted it all the time, it was worth it, it was big and beautiful and she wanted all the time and, Daddy, oh thank you thank you thank you thank you Daddy was in there and Daddy made it bigger, smaller, wider, narrower, changing, ever changing, finding every contour of the cunt that was taking it in. Ooooh. Deep into the mattress her back was sinking. Skin on skin, skin on silk, body on body, she could move with, she could shift with, she could take it, she could take it and she could sink, she could sink oh so deep.

And she sank on through the mattress and she sank on through the floor and she sank on through the foundation and she sank and sank and sank and sank. Bodies still intertwined, they fell as if cast out from some far-off nebulous Heaven, into something and somewhere, in the dark beneath the very earth. A cavern, a sanctum, a space of deconsecrated sanctity. Falling and falling as one, they landed through the night into a room aglow with crimson as if lit by many invisible sconces and beneath it all, a deep, still lake of rich, dark red, like a giant pool of pulsing, sighing, living burgundy. There were lives down there, maybe life in the water itself.

They plunged, they splashed, and the blood, the red flowed into her mouth and her eyes, sticky, coppery sweet but with a tinge of meat to it, glurping and bubbling into her body by every route it could. It clung. A slick clot snaked around her legs, then began to climb, venturing between them, winding up, then sliding all the way into her, exciting regions of desire she had no idea she'd wanted. Cassilda had known such comfort and pleasure that it was almost hard to accept what was coming into her.

It was thirst but not just thirst, strength that was not

just strength. The world was new, not just for smoking, eating, and fucking. The world was filled with squeaking, bleating prey, filthy and ignorant beasts that it would be ever so easy to overcome. She had had compassion and a need for love before, but she was wrong in this; there were but two things that mattered: Daddy's love and the consumption of innocent blood.

BRIDAL SUITE

Opium black, thick as all things, thick as all things that existed. It was warm and cool at once, pervasive and pregnant with promise. Pup was in a darkness for floating in, the void, perhaps the one from which love emanated, the bottom of Pandora's box in which the hope was stored. The night had wrapped Pup in this ancient, cozy cloak, and Pup could just be. For Pup to just be was a rare thing that had been a bit more common before before before …

Couldn't be right. The world was a quiet, dark, and gentle place, unburdened by noise or woe or violence or bigotry or any number of words Pup did not think that they could ever not think. Wherever Pup was, Pup was as glad as could be to be there, taken by someone good and kind and gentle into a place of solace and reflection.

"I bring you here," said a voice in the dark, "because you deserve a place of love and joy and hope in your scary and stressful life. I brought you because you said you needed a place to live. So I have given you one. So what do you say to that, Pup?"

"Thank you," said Pup. Pup now remembered that

prior to this, they had struggled to find a place to sleep and they had gone somewhere where they met a kind and handsome and powerful man who gave them a soft, cool, and comfortable place where they could stay. This man was as strong as he was caring, and there was nothing Pup could think of that they would not do for Daddy. It was happening fast, but love was love, and love without need was something Pup had craved their whole life. Possibly. Was there a time when Pup didn't have—

"I want you to remember a good doggie, Pup," said the voice in the opiate void. "I want you to show me and share with me what it is to be a good doggie."

Pup could not reach many memories but could reach for some warmth and some light and some hope. Pup found it where they had found it during years of hostile adults and absence of, of … of something that was harder to reach than the memory of the loyal, loving, and ever vigilant black and white dog. Pup held the dog tight and faded into this love. Millie was a source of goodness and delight; Millie was love unconditional and a thing Pup aspired to be.

"Such a good doggie," said Daddy's voice in the dark. "Will you be a good doggie for me, Pup?"

"Yes," said Pup, beaming at the chance to find the dog again in the pitch-black peaceful nonplace and at the dream of making Daddy happy.

"It has been too long since I have had a dog. I have four wives, but I did not have a dog, and there was a great, loveless void wherein there would have been a dog. A home without a dog is hardly a home at all; wouldn't you say?"

Pup thought again of Millie, a thought that was permitted here in this darkness. Millie had made that house almost a home, almost liveable in spite of in spite of … in spite of something that could not shine through in these clouds of oblivion. A house was not a home without a dog, and it would be a shame if this was no home, as this was to be Pup's home. Pup would serve as a very good doggie in this home. Pup wanted most to be a very good doggie.

In the dark, there was touch, hands stroking up and down Pup's back, rubbing and toying with Pup's hair. These hands were not Daddy's; they were softer, soft as the concealing night, the shadowy bed sheet womb where Pup was floating. They grazed, tickled gently. Breath behind Pup's ear. A tiny nibble. A sudden playful pinch on the ass. A single, solitary frame of brush by phantasmal lips on Pup's cheek. There was no counting the number of gentle hands and teasing lips, no counting the shapes concealed by this dark around Pup. Pup was surrounded but surrounded by passion, surrounded by gentleness and affirmation and peace.

"Who …?" Pup asked before there emerged a sultry face with a caring but mischievous gaze. Then shadow parted like a curtain, like clothes ripped away to reveal a pair of fake but sublimely round breasts, unhampered by gravity, borne way by a wan body. Walking on legs more slender than these curves anticipated and sporting a surprisingly hard, confident erection. Pup had met a few Thai ladyboys at clubs and had thought their bodies resembled presurgical photos of Lenore. This young woman was a perfect example of the aesthetic and the body, impossibly tall on very high heels.

"Do you want to kiss it?" she asked breathily. Pup wanted very much to kiss it, the smooth ideal girlcock that they had dreamed of since first seeing it on Pornhub.

Pup licked it gently, nervously at first, then fervently, taking in the contours, the mix of soft and hard that would feel just so perfect inside. Licking it was nice, but it was good to have it inside. As Pup began, another pair of hands held firm on their ass and then cupped their testicles, not squeezing but gently toying, treating them like the pearls they felt like. There was something bigger, stranger, and more perfect than reality in their touch and encounter, but it was fine, and Pup had nothing but gratitude for it, nothing but gratitude for Daddy for giving the experience.

"I … I …" Pup said to the bearer of the perfect girl cock. "I need …"

Pup didn't see her coming up from behind, but there she was, sliding effortlessly into Pup, abandoning both lube and reason to the velvety instrument sliding inside. Pup moved into the sensation as they had with Daddy, finding their body more eager and pliant than they had ever dreamed of. Pup let the ladyboy sink herself in and get comfortable, feeling the pain, the pleasure, the inward tingling of use. The rough parts were there when Pup needed them but then gone when they didn't. A tiny glimpse of Lenore's gifts with the strap blinked into Pup's mind, letting nostalgia tint the delight of skilled and tender sodomy.

"Good doggie," she whispered from behind him. "This is for you because Daddy loves us. Daddy loves us all so much; you know that? You need to let Daddy in; you need to let him stay. Let me in, let Daddy in, let love in. Can you let love back in, Pup?"

"I want …" said a confused and heated Pup. "I want to let love back in. I want to live with and to give love. I want to be kind and unconditionally loving, like a dog. I want to be the doggie."

A tall, thick redhead, pale save for dozens of inscrutable tattoos, was previously behind Pup but seemed to instantly switch places, scooping Pup's face in her hands for a deep kiss, all the while toying with, yanking on Pup's nipples until they got nice and hard. A lot of Pup was getting nice and hard. It was a strange whirl, a blur of experience drawing Pup to the outer edge of it. Hard-on intense, knees shaking hard, Pup was confused and overexcited, uncertain of what they wanted when suddenly, an unfamiliar blonde appeared and made something a bit more clear in the haze. Pup wanted them all for as long as he could have them and wanted that fantastic girldick deep the whole time, but Pup was hungry and needy and changed, changed perhaps by the sight of the blonde.

The blonde was half doe-eyed submission, half the kind of hunger that could destroy her and anything it touched. She walked into this pocket of night, and a spotlight off in the distance seemed to shine on her, even with the two beauties occupying Pup's attention. She was bright, so bright, mouth agape. She stroked her face and body as if they were new to her, exploring the softness. She reached down between her legs, pulling out a finger to find that she was wet already, even if that finger was daubed with blood, which she sucked from it with breathy enthusiasm. The ecstasy of her body was infectious from first sight. It was so very kind of Daddy to provide this place and the promise of touch like this. So much satisfaction to be had and shared here.

"You're pretty," said the blonde. "Daddy said he'd got a doggie. But he didn't say you'd be so pretty. Goddamn, you're so pretty. I don't think I can stand it."

A tear streamed down her cheek and stained it red. The redhead broke their kiss to let out a sigh, a pant, a tiny growl, then renewed the kiss, bit down on Pup's lip until it bled. It didn't hurt too bad, though, it hurt nice, and she seemed like she really needed it. When she pulled away, Pup noticed that the lip wasn't bleeding at all, not a drop. She twitched just a bit, shuddered, almost overcome by just the tiny little taste, the tiny little taste that promised so much more. She looked Pup over, then smiled as she shook her head. She had made some decision or another, but it was difficult to tell just what it was. Even if Pup could, there was a smooth, perfect cock playing their body as an instrument, building a conduit, starting a machine that powered Pup and their own erection, which would find purpose and delight in this structure that they were to build together.

"Can you fuck me, please?" said the blonde. "I'm so excited, so confused, and I feel so empty. I need someone in me. Can you be inside me? I need it; I really fucking need it."

"Ruff," said Pup.

The blonde knew to lie down, slide towards Pup, spread her legs, and smile invitingly. There was no thought of pregnancy, disease, death, safety. Just as Pup had let the cock inside, Pup adjusted themself, got on top, back still arched, and then slid inside of the blonde. She was sopping, wringing wet somehow, and though her juices were thicker than pussy juice and thicker than lube, stickier, more solid, Pup still found it easy to enter her, easy to fuck her. She was tight and inviting, sucking him right in as if it were a second mouth instead of a vagina. Pup pulsed with the friction, the ease, and the moistness, moved with it, soaked it up, and thrust with an excitement that had not been there for some time, a comfort with an organ that they did not think of or employ that often and that they did not feel like using like this. But Pup was in.

The redhead took another nibble of Pup's lip, biting harder, latching on, and still sucking. The pain this time was greater, but that was settled on the lovely, enticing, and body-shaking task at hand, on the machine that took and gave all at once, connecting these bodies as one formidable and fully charged thing, an instrument of self-realization and fulfilment that overlooked the agony and the problems and the dark that this all happened in, the sordid circumstances that had brought them together not even for a second prodding at them. There could be no doubt of each other's inner lives or motives for this act; they were there, transparent, and easy. It was all so easy for once. There were only bodies to think of and what they could give and get.

Pup could be happy like this. Pup could be safe like this. There may have been other things Pup wanted besides the conduit of fucking and getting fucked, the covenant of mouths and bodies, the promises between lovers that are sealed with all that's in them, that they anoint as sanctuary with fluids and moans and uttermost essences. Pup was where they needed to be, and rarest and most relevant of all, Pup was where they wanted to stay. Each pump taken, each pump given, each pump whispered to the universe and the only one whose opinion on the matter was relevant, "Please don't make me go, please let me be here, please let me be yours, it means so much to be yours."

Intertwined, they carried on, at once each other's so completely and yet still all Daddy's, residing in Daddy's void in Daddy's home, where none could bring scrutiny or doubt or fear. There was no anguish, only fuck; there were no mysteries or distractions, only fuck. Fuck was life and fuck was law, and fuck travelled back and forth through skin and veins and mouths and genitals, making its strength asserted. If the sun should blot out or the seas should rise, still there would be bodies and with those bodies, exploration and pleasure and intensity and delight. Pup held on as long as they could, wishing to prolong this so they might inhabit this moment with these beautiful and adoring bodies sealing a circle of what might have been but did not need to be love.

There was anticipation, and the first feeling that could be called negative was a tinge of fear and regret. It was only the fear of the terminus of something perfect; it was only the regret that it was not about to start over again and repeat and repeat and repeat until this was all they ever had to know or do again. This was the shadow of doubt, this was fear's intrusion, and even in this, there was the excitement of impending climax, the build toward something that many saw as part and parcel point and purpose of the act. If the closest thing Pup felt to dread was the knowledge that they were going to cum, then they were at their safest and luckiest, lucky Pup.

Hands, mouths, cock, and cunt alike whispered encouragement and ushered it onward to the brink of something else, something sublime. Pup felt a twitch, a harder, more determined thrust than the others before, a scream from the hips that, in a massive spurt, made clear what these movements were saying. They were saying be ready, they were saying thank you, and they were saying, "This is for you, baby, this is what you have wrought and what you've given. Take it, take it, please." It was thicker than any load Pup had taken before, again with an unusual viscosity and opacity not unlike that of the juice in the blonde's cunt. It was strange, but it was vibrant, substantive, and electric. Pup's body responded in the most likely of ways.

Pup tensed and clenched and soaked up the incoming explosion of cum, and their own hips gave an urgent and histrionic spasm, an ur-thrust of tightening and loosening muscles doing that which they wanted most to do in a body that they wanted so much to give pleasure to that all behind it were hazy, all behind it living outside this great veil of quiet, nonjudgmental night, a darkness that made all deeds and desires explicable and excusable. And in this place and in this time and with those obsessions, there was but the one recourse, alpha becoming tintinnabulant omega.

Clenched. Shook. Thrust. Came. A tightness and all to gleam from hope and dream and testicles and heart came spilling forth, past clouds and walls of needed repression.

"Fill me, that's it," said the blonde, "fill me."

Pup filled her until Pup was empty, though still full of the fluids that the splendid girlcock had put there. Pup collapsed and held her until they felt the redhead's impossibly firm and strong hands roll them off. The redhead then got down on her knees and began to violently lick and suck at the fresh load in the blonde, taking in the fluids as though they were life itself, which unbeknownst to Pup, they certainly were. Broad tongue strokes and fevered sucking sought to get all she could from the scene of this great explosion of shared passions. She swallowed hard, then pulled away, proudly showing a face stained the color and texture of a strawberry milkshake. The dark, sultry trans woman kissed it off, kissed it clean, shared the lust.

Sighing, huffing, Pup felt pain catch up until it took its leave again. Daddy's face, then the rough hands of a strange bald man leading them down an impossibly long staircase.

PUP IN THE BIG ROOM

The mattress Pup had been led to was firm but unadorned. The room was no place and the atmosphere nothing. A warehouse, perhaps, or a basement. Mattress and grey concrete and mattress and a whole lot of dank, grey, and unfocused nothing. Some crates or something would have helped lend the place a firmer sense of identity, but there was dusty, grey empty instead. The void had felt comforting and consoling, wrapping Pup in arms of mystery. This was no longer that thing. This room was something else, as firmly planted in consensus reality as that had not been.

It was nice that beside the mattress, there were edibles and some poppers, Xanax, three butt plugs adorned with various animal tails. It was difficult for Pup to tell if they were dealing with an absolute savage that had—no, never—if they were dealing with a—no never—or if they were under the care of a truly benign and generous and wonderful benefactor. There were other mattresses and other people on them, but it was hard for Pup to feel interested in them, not when Daddy was out there being the beautiful and magical creature Daddy was. Pup would get to know them, surely friends of Daddy's, but let themself feel the languid and joyful sensation of being Daddy's.

There was also, on a mattress about a foot away, a shamelessly naked woman, body a great plain of lush, thick flesh that called out for touch and kisses and unabashed, ecstatic fucking. Though lust had just been fulfilled and slaked, Pup couldn't help but feel it renewed, especially on account of the open, generous way she lay in repose, an offering of her lushness for all the eyes in the room to feast upon. Pup could join her on that mattress and maybe could go again with just a taste. It would be nice to have just a taste. Maybe a couple gummies or a pill and then … so much, it was just so much. So many drugs, so much flesh, so much power and generosity.

"You're new," said a voice from across the room, a female voice that Pup's eyes followed. "Are you afraid yet?"

Pup turned and faced the questioner. Her skin was dark and rich; her hair was wild, an organized tangle of cultivated and well-loved chaos—if one looked at it for long enough, there were things to divine from the shapes, like candle wax or tea leaves. She was the physical opposite of the woman on the mattress beside Pup's. Looking at the two, one could almost think that they had been selected by a decorator's eye to create a sense of symmetry. The young woman was wearing no pants or skirt, just a tight t-shirt with a ravenous purple shark on it, and her eyes were looking past the room to somewhere or something impossibly far. She was looking through and not at Pup, a gaze that only looked through things. Pup was scared, but in spite of all the overstimulation and all of the things that could have seemed suspicious, Pup was fascinated.

"I don't know," said Pup. "I've seen some weird things, but they were so beautiful and it all feels so good. It feels like some beautiful dream. Are you part of some beautiful dream?"

"I am," she said. "I am in and of his dream. You are in and of his dream. You have felt him, you have felt them, so you know. Cassilda had another name once. She had friends and a home and so much to think about. She's happier now, I think."

A small, squat, strong man in a black tank top and shorts, likely trans, sat up on a nearby mattress.

"I'm sorry about Asha," he said. "She's losing her mind."

"Asha," said the fleshy divinity nearby, "Asha knows things. Asha is seeing through all this and might be giving up."

"That's awful," said Pup, not grasping what the notion of surrender entailed or what there was to surrender to.

"Surrender is not a thing to lament. Surrender is beautiful. You wouldn't be here if you didn't know that," said Asha, "if you didn't know the virtue of surrender. In surrender, every prisoner is free. You can be happy if you put your mind to it. That's in a song my mother used to sing."

A slender, long-legged crane of a woman with a great shock of blue hair rose up from another nearby mattress as if hearing something shocking. Her face was cute but angular, her hips square. The angles and curves of typical femininity eluded her, but there was an air to her, a softness, a willingness, and an eagerness that was like that of the bigger woman but different somehow, a product of dream unfulfilled and of a thirst for something else.

"You remember your mother, Asha?" she asked, shocked.

"I remember the song," said Asha. "When I take my pills, I can hear it. You can't drive around with a tiger in your car, you know?"

"I do know that," said Pup. "It would be really dangerous."

"I think Asha doesn't know what the fuck she's saying," said the guy, who Pup was now certain was trans and had a hot rockabilly vibe.

"It's you," said Asha, "who doesn't know what the fuck I'm saying. I'm looking at amazing things and learning a lot. I give you gold, it ain't my fault you don't recognize it, Lex."

"It's a little your fault," said the blue-haired girl with an endearing smile.

"I'm Pup," said Pup, smiling back at the blue-haired girl. "I'm new."

"I know," she said with a very free giggle on the end of it. "I haven't seen you around, Pup. I noticed the ears. I like 'em."

Pup felt almost shy. These people were pretty; these people seemed cool. Pup liked them. Pup liked everything and everyone here. It was nice that Daddy had brought Pup to meet and stay with these nice people because Daddy was so thoughtful and so good. There were all these nice things for Pup to do and take. Maybe these people liked to fuck. Pup could fuck any of these people. Pup would fuck all of them. Fuck. They should fuck. It would be so hot if they fucked. Daddy would probably like it if they fucked. Pup bet they'd fuck if Pup asked.

"Thanks," said Pup, instead of *Let's fuck, let's fuck right now, I need to fuck you all, I need it so much, fuck, we have to fuck, I'm empty and it hurts and I need to be touched and I need to be ready for next time that I need to fuck, fuck, please, I need it.*

The blue-haired woman approached and sat down on the mattress, scritching Pup's head. She kissed their face, then took a good long look at it, and Pup in turn looked at hers. She was not perfect, not by a long shot, but she was perfect. She was not as long transitioned as Lenore had been, nor as comfortable in her body, but she was happy and she was eager, and there was a wonderful air of giving about her. The others, there was something sad that was clear to see, but this one, so calm, so gentle, and so generous with her touch, was something else. She reminded Pup of the intensity of the three perfect women. Fuck, that was so nice.

"You're really cute, Pup," said the blue-haired woman. "I'm Houston. You feel nice."

"I do," said Pup. "I feel really nice."

Pup could see Lenore's face, remember Lenore's comfort, felt tinges of Lenore's loss, but fondly recalled times they had been brought to places like this to meet folks like this. Lenore had such cool friends, and now Pup was going to have such cool friends. Lenore was gone and that was bad, but Pup had Daddy now, and it was so good to have Daddy. Lenore could not compare to Daddy. It would be okay to forget Lenore.

"We try not to fuck here," said the cute trans guy with the rockabilly vibe. "It's what he wants."

Pup wanted to fuck that guy. It would be so nice to feel that body loosening up and giving way to pleasure, to see those dark, intense eyes finding calm in the storm of a very rough life. It would be nice if they could cum together, especially if it would make Daddy happy. Pup wanted what Daddy wanted. Pup was loyal, Pup was loving, Pup was Daddy's Pup and would do anything to make Daddy happy, particularly if it meant doing some fucking. Pup should have felt exhausted from the three women, but instead Pup felt excited, invigorated, and ready to experience these bodies.

"We try," said Asha, with an odd, creaking door of a smile, "but we don't always manage."

"What brought you guys here?" Pup asked, trying

to get away from the feelings of lust building up or the feelings of embarrassment at the feelings of lust.

"I don't really remember," said Houston.

"We talk," said the bib woman Pup would come to know as Luna, "but somehow, there never seems to be all that much to talk about."

Pup thought that sounded weird. Everyone here was so kind, so beautiful, and seemed to care about one another. Why would they be so bored of each other? Pup felt a tinge of disquiet. Something could have been wrong. There were questions, something held back those questions, but for a second, that something was flimsier. Why was Daddy being so generous? What was this place? Who was who was who was surely there was a who was surely there was a good explanation.

"Sometimes, you get the fears," said Asha, "but don't worry too much about that. It will come and it will go. You'll be called on, and then you'll be called back. You'll do your business, then you'll come back, and everything you need will be here. It's not a bad life, far as I remember."

Suddenly, Pup felt quite sure it wasn't.

MISSING PERSONS

"I'll bite you, sweetheart," Lenore had said, "but I won't break skin; you understand?"

Christian had wondered if this was a metaphor. He looked back on it, and he remembered how likely it was that he was going to fall in love with her. He remembered her body against him, the feel of that body, at once slight and toned and strong, pressed against him, making him happier than his wife ever had, than his comfort and his job and the good life he had worked for ever had. He really could have given all those things up; he was telling the truth there. But maybe she could tell that and wished he wouldn't. She bit him on the shoulder as she slid the strap-on in, light and measured, but it hit just right. She didn't break skin.

Alone, jerking off in his condo and wondering what to make of himself, he often returned to that time with Lenore and her strap and her passion. He thought often about how she'd bite him but she wouldn't break skin, a commitment she could hit the precipice of but would not cross, just like his to the life he really wanted. He didn't like the thought of that half so much as he liked the feel of Lenore in him and on him. But Lenore was gone, from his life, from poor Pup's. Lenore might have momentarily brought Christian to lust; his mind and heart fell into grief, not just for the part of his life she took with her but for the woman he had loved.

Christian contemplated the beers in the fridge. He'd already smoked a bowl, and it wasn't making his life any easier, but maybe a couple cold ones could. He contemplated maybe instead going out and finding a place where he could have a cold drink. Maybe he could meet someone there. Maybe he could bring that someone back to the condo and he could be fucked by and fuck them and he could be the person he was when Dana was out of town. Dana was only at work. There wouldn't be much time, and if there was evidence, he would have to explain that. He needed something more immediate and more visceral. Decided instead that he would get out of the house and hook up.

Christian made it all the way to the car with his mind on the adult video store on 82nd and its gloryholes, where there were cocks and mouths to be found pretty much anytime. He could almost feel himself on his knees exalting in the service of the cock presented to him and of the knowledge that he was free and clear and there was nobody there who would judge him, not like Dana, who he knew could never understand and would be broken if she saw this side of him. He had to protect her, but he had already given so much of his life and his satisfaction keeping her safe from who he was and what he wanted. He could be her husband, but he would need to be someone else from time to time.

He felt that need to be someone else today. He felt tempted to become that person and never come back to the life he had sacrificed so much to get. He could disappear into the bodies and the touch and the validation that these things offered and the inward glow of authenticity that the life presented. It would be better if he could be authentic with the people he'd built a life with, but he had made his choice and his trade. He could turn around and go back to regarding himself as someone's husband and handle the emails from his clients, but he wasn't going to do that. He was going to let the thirst for touch and affirmation bear him southeast toward anonymous blowjobs and safe, manageable fear, fear that tightened your balls but did not pull you away.

He bought a Gatorade at the corner store, got a couple fives as cashback for the arcade machine in case the stay got long. Did the lady at the Fred Meyer know where he was headed, or was he just feeling the eyes of his wife upon him? She was judging and had good reason; she wanted him to turn back from this, turn back from being this other person he was. If the clerk knew, then maybe she could, maybe she would, yes, it was possible, yes, it could have been that she would report back to—no, no. Getting paranoid. Head together. This is just a trip to the fuckbooth. There is nothing worth deep scrutiny for. He was going to the fuckbooth to fuck, and then he would be okay and easier to live with and less depressed, and everyone wanted that, even those who didn't know because he didn't tell them.

He parked in front of the video store, got out, and walked inside. He minced around past dozens of naked bodies on display on DVD covers and dozens of toys, costumes, and instruments of every imaginable size. This was a place that housed imagination and magic in spite of its crass facade, a place whose wares transformed the world, manifesting scenes that had been confined to dreams and dark and private wishes cooked up in the mind when sleep danced, tempting at the edge of eyelids, promising caress but withdrawing, never giving in. There were wonders and perverse miracles within, and they could be manifested by the daring. He paced around as if pretending that he was going to choose one, that his life was so rich with pervy accomplices that he could make French maid inflatable sheep orgies happen with a snap of his fingers.

Eventually, he gave up his short, performative examination of the wares, which was as much to show he wasn't just going back to the arcade to shoot up as to pay lip service to the masters of the house. He went into that hallway, avoiding the theater space in favor of the intimacy of the fuckbooth, and while he knew there were not going to be any particularly good catches, he would at least be getting the much-needed taste of his lifestyle that he found here and feel fully realized. That was a lot more important than building a hot scene with an individual he wouldn't have touched with a ten-foot pole. He put a five into the machine and loaded up a twink getting fucked by a long line of grey-bearded muscle men, power bottom held aloft to receive.

He could have pulled out his cock and slid it into the hole and waited for whatever would happen, but Dana sucked him off sometimes, and she was solidly tight. There was something he couldn't get at home, and he decided that should take priority, so he got down on his knees and leaned at the hole, mouth open and waiting for confirmation that he was an acknowledged part of this, a real and sexy object deserving an entire spectrum of treatment from rough to loving, dependent upon how he chose to get it and from whom. On his knees, he was making a prayer to please be that person that fell for Lenore and find the love and joy that had brought him, or at least … a taste. Wouldn't be the same, couldn't, but he needed at least to get closer.

There was nothing for a few minutes, long enough that he had to toss some more cash into the machine, which was already moving onto a new and different and barely related porno. In this purgatory, his knees were getting a little sore, but he braced himself, knowing that this was the sacrifice sluts went through. He hadn't had it for a week. He could have sucked Pup off, but Pup didn't really give that vibe. Pup was on the other end of the hole, and that was how that went. Pup wanted to please, so Christian could have asked but wasn't going to do that to someone who had lost as much as Pup had, more even than Christian, at the death of Lenore. In a perfect world, Lenore's cock would come through that hole and she would be laughing. She would say, "I got you homos good!" But this wasn't a perfect world.

This world was good enough at least to furnish Christian with a reasonable length of meat that he could wrap his mouth around and close his eyes and feel the girth and the gag in veneration as thrust and thrust and thrust asserted he was whore and not just husband, more than he'd had credit for and more than he gave himself. With heavy hips and rage at life, the man on the other end gave Christian's mouth the workout it desired, lasting several drooling, near puking minutes more than either had hoped it would but culminating finally in a nice, big, anonymous mouthful that said to him, "Yes, you're who you are, my god, you've done it, you fucking cumdump, you're real and you're okay."

He breathed heavily, wiped his mouth, got out, and, winded, found his way to his car. He ate four Altoids in short order, got a Coke and a chicken sandwich from the Popeye's drive-through on the way home to cleanse his palate, and relaxed with the rush of sneaking out to serve cock in the middle of the day, sucking off someone he would not have given the time of day or perhaps would have crossed the street to avoid. On 82nd, it was more likely to be the latter than the former. It felt good to know it was more likely the latter than the former, something sketchy, clandestine, and weird, something that made him want to keep trying to maintain the balance.

Most of the way home, he thought of Pup again and texted them.

"You good?"

There was no reply. It was possible that the phone was off or the phone bill unpaid, but Christian knew what the crowd and the scene could be like sometimes and knew that Lenore would have wanted him to follow up, and even if Lenore was gone, he should keep the best of Lenore in him as best he could. Pup knew that's what people do for those they love. He waited and worried until getting back to his laptop and opening up FetLife. There was a group on there for the club, and he could scan it for the people he knew through Lenore; maybe one of them who'd checked into the event would have seen Pup. Maybe Christian should have reached out to begin with and explained that Pup was Lenore's sub and needed a place. Fuck. That would have been the right thing to do.

He found an old friend of Lenore's and sent her a ping.

"Hey, I'm Christian. We met at bi night one time. I'm a friend of Lenore's and concerned because her sub is not replying to texts and hasn't posted on the gram or anything for over a week. Have you seen Pup around?"

The one message wouldn't be enough. Christian went through three more of Lenore's old acquaintances and a couple of his own. There were a lot of longshots that Christian didn't try outright because he was worried about looking like a creep or a stalker. It was pretty likely that could happen, but it mattered more if it got in the way of his old obligation to Lenore, now dead. He glanced through the long rows of photos on those pages, saw some moments with Lenore, saw some moments he wished he'd been part of, saw how much of his life was a lie once again, even though that wasn't the important part. This was supposed to be about Pup and not about that creeping emptiness.

He sat in that creeping emptiness, in that sensation that he had let too many things that mattered slip away from him. What if he had gone with Lenore and insisted she not meet up with that last john? Maybe he could have kept Lenore around if he was honest with his wife, and then from there, Lenore would have gotten to survive. Fuck. If Pup hadn't lived, he would have wronged Lenore again, he would have been the wrong one to live through it yet another time, and he would have left yet another sad, broken body behind him in the wake of his self-deception and insincerity.

Four pings that said, "I'm sorry, never met them." A bunch of messages un-replied-to. An utter lack of news faced him, along with the phantoms of his own grief and misery and doubt preparing to drag him into a lonesome sensory hell. He wanted more from himself. Lenore would have wanted more from him than to try and fail and be stonewalled by too many of the people he couldn't truly be one of. Face in hands, he was ready to give up before his laptop pinged out another answer.

"I know who you're talking about. Needed a place to stay, went home with Daddy."

There were a lot of people who called themselves Daddy, but Christian knew they meant Le Comte. Daddy was a whisper in the night; Daddy was an ugly rumor and an unstoppable reality. Daddy was a staircase of broken stairs and Santa Claus with dragons in his bag. If Christian wanted to find Pup, he would have to find Daddy. He very much didn't want to find Daddy.

BARKING IN THE NIGHT

A new day began with Pup finding themself in no place in particular—if it was a new day. Whatever the building had been, it was so completely Daddy's that Daddy chose which room was which and what happened inside them. Pup was in a room, a windowless room, featureless too, a little pocket of nothing but a bed. In this world, this cosmos of Daddy's, the bed was the sole feature that all of them shared, as deserts had sand and forests had trees, every room that was Daddy's had a mattress, since there was nothing that Daddy wanted from Pup that could not have been done on that mattress. Pup was too drunk with excitement to regret or despair at that notion, rather, ready to exalt in it.

There was a ring, a veritable forest of hard, eager cocks that dangled from the men in Daddy's crew, and Pup was quickly on hands and knees at the center of it. There was violent desperation in their eyes as they jerked to keep themselves at full stock, all worried, it seemed, about getting too excited. Pup did not need to be told what was going on or ordered to suck these men off. Pup was dog, and dog was love; Pup was

Daddy's, and Daddy must have been the one to bring them all together. If it was Daddy that brought them all together, then Pup needed to bring anyone they were given to pleasure. Pup jerked and licked and sucked these men, hungrily lapping and then moving on to full-on deepthroating.

A fugue of harm. Something was coming up, but the ones using Pup's face weren't listening. Pup could feel the vomit getting fucked back down from whence it came, and the consequences were obvious. The men were indefatigable in their hunger to use Pup, the leader finally taking a turn at Pup's ass when Pup was feeling just barely capable of holding back from throwing up on the cock in their mouth. The leader was digging nails deep into Pup's hips, stopping to periodically spit on their semi-willing fuckdoll's bare back. Jizz and saliva, streaks of blood. Purpling slaps on the face. This is love. This is a gift. Every day of Daddy's love is a fresh, new gift.

Life faded until Pup was hobbling downstairs, the bigger, broader, unknowable world behind them, along with almost all memory of the figures and events from the past few godawful minutes, godawful hours. Had there been a railing before? Perhaps there had. Pup had never recalled going downstairs. Lex and Houston met them halfway, brought them down to towel them off and share some painkillers. The two hovered over Pup to bring some aid and comfort to their injured roommate.

"You're bleeding. They could have killed you," said Lex. "They went too far again."

"They get excited," said Houston. "They're using what Daddy gives them."

"They have to keep you down," said Asha. "There's something in you they see that needs to be stomped and snuffed and reduced to nothing. You're special,

Pup. I don't say that to nobody."

"Thanks, Asha," said Pup, and meant it. Luna and Houston finished the cleaning and tending to the injuries of the day, and Pup lay down to rest; idly, perhaps but Pup needed that sleep.

Pup, however, could not sleep. Muscles, lungs, ass, they were hurting, which could have been fixed by the Xanax or the edibles or whatever the fuck else was in that bottle, but Pup wasn't going to. This was different. The room was ice. The room was blue. Pup's limbs were numb. Pup could not move. And in the moonlight in the middle of this windowless room stood a creature that had once been a dog. The mattresses and the occupants had somehow disappeared and left behind the chill and the glow and the creature that had once been a dog. It approached, and Pup was filled with dread and panic. Not a dog anymore. Consistent in its inconsistency; in spots, grey-green and gelatinous; in spots, tough as leather; well done steak held together with ragged spancels of black and white fur pasted to its body by the run of decomposition.

The eyes gave it away, or at least gave away its falsity. Pup did not like the implication.

"You're not Millie," Pup said, finding they could speak even if they couldn't move. "You're a trick; someone's tricking me."

"You are as right as you are wrong," said NotMillie. "In death, we're not what we were. You'd do well to remember. Death is coming if you don't use The Face Beneath. She gave a gift, connected us."

Pup tried to shake off the nightmare. There was a way out. Pup had seen shadows, a Hatman, other artifacts of sleep paralysis. This was that, it was surely that, this rotten mockery of their beloved dog suddenly gifted with speech, just for words of torment.

"Why do you look like that?" Pup asked.

"Dog is love," said NotMillie, "and in this place, love lies broken. We howled at monsters in the night for the people that loved us first. You are now among monsters, and the howl comes from The Face Beneath. You were given a gift, a connection renewed. You know she wouldn't leave you."

"There is no skin on you," said Pup.

"I've been sent," said NotMillie, "to show you what she wants you to see."

In the middle of the room, a car appeared. Pup found their limbs available suddenly; Pup found themself standing up. NotMillie stood by the car and waited dutifully as she had waited for Pup when she was still called Millie. Pup moved through clouds of azure moonglow to the car where the corpsedog was waiting. Inside was Lenore; inside with Lenore was a man with careworn skin that had a texture reminiscent of a cheap wallet. Just looking at him, Pup could smell him. Lenore's tits were out; it was clear what was going on here.

"I don't need to see this," said Pup to NotMillie.

"Then why," said the dog, warm border collie eyes fixed tight, "do you think you're seeing it?"

"You're not Millie," Pup repeated.

"I am dog," said NotMillie, "and we are kin. Watch and understand."

Pup hesitantly looked back into that window at Lenore and the john. There was only one moment this could be, and that moment meant loveless, meant ruin, meant empty and hollow and gone, gone, and nothing could be good and nothing could be safe and nothing would really matter, not really, and nothing could be planned more than a day ahead. Pup watched and Pup listened, hearing as if they were right in the back of the car.

"Do you remember a man named Schaffer?"

"I don't think I knew a Schaffer, sweetheart," said Lenore with a nervous smile. And Lenore should have opened the door of the car and come back to Pup, who loved her and missed her and needed her all the time.

Lenore did not. Lenore should have shoved his head against the window, burst through the door, and fled back to Pup, who loved and missed her so much and would cuddle and kiss and treasure her, but she didn't and couldn't stand a chance against this angry man with his shining knife, gleaming in the night. Silver. It was silver, shining metallic and then shining dark and slick with the blood of the love of Pup's life, with the spray of the life that had made Pup's life worth living.

"This is for my brother!" the john screamed as he murdered her. She was dead about halfway through the barrage of stabs, but this man, eyes filled with tears, kept going, kept desecrating Lenore. "This is for my brother." What the fuck could that mean? Pup had never known Lenore to hurt anyone, save for a face full of pepper spray or a kick in the junk if things got rough.

Pup broke down and cried. This was so fucked up. This was so completely wrong. This demon with Pup had come forth wearing the body of the dog Pup had loved most in the world, the only creature that had made life worth anything in that house Pup couldn't remember from this place and wouldn't if they could choose to. First mocking the death of this beloved pet, this Love as Pup understood it, and then the death of Pup's deepest, truest love. How could Daddy allow such a thing to happen here?

"Why? I'm already so confused down here. I don't understand any of this. I don't know if Daddy loves or hates me. Why do you have to fuck with me when I'm down in a basement surrounded by scared strangers? What kind of fucking monster does this to someone?"

"My intent is not to break you down," said NotMillie.

"It is to show you what you need to survive everything ahead. Do you know what the man who holds you captive is?"

Pup nodded, pushing past the tears. Suddenly, there was the notion that Pup was someone's captive and not someone's adored and comforted pet. The abuse from the crew should have been enough, but this night visitor was helping to cut through the mass of bizarre ideas that was starting to collect in Pup's mind. Something was wrong about Daddy. Daddy had done some things that were ugly, some things that were scary.

"I think he might not be human. I think he can do things people can't. Asha says he's more than human and too powerful to resist."

The fleshless dog leaned her face against Pup's leg, and while, physically, it felt wrong and grotesque, there was an air of familiarity, an air of hope, of love. While the exact moments were as hard to pick out as most memories of the world before this place, the sensation and what it meant were still abundantly clear. There was a reason Pup had become Pup, a reason this dog was a model of love.

"He is monstrous," said the fleshless dog. "Dog is love, but love will not be enough. A gift was given. You will need to make use of it."

Pup watched themself standing in Lenore's arms. Lenore was tall as Pup and not shy about the heels. Lenore had a name before Lenore and soft grey eyes and that sharp, intricate face that could be so severe but also so very kind. Pup was forgetting, which this place tried hard to do, but in this bright moonlit place, this ghost place, Lenore was there. Lenore placed her head on Pup's shoulder, and Pup now remembered something that felt like they would never forget it.

Lenore tilted Pup's face up, kissed Pup fierce, kissed deep, mad, urgent, strong as tide and time. Pup could almost feel that kiss, almost. Pup could feel the need to feel that kiss. Pup could feel the need to feel Lenore clamping down, at first gentle, on Pup's shoulder, then biting deep, and Pup, while sure they could not speak to object, did bark, the anguished bark, the shocked bark, the "that's too hard" bark, and while Lenore would usually stop biting from there, the bite didn't stop, the bite didn't give, and the skin, the skin was broken, which was like but unlike Lenore. The bark ended; the pain gave way to some kind of ecstasy at being so used and making Lenore so horny and so happy.

Lenore pulled away, held Pup, and kissed them again. Her eyes were teary, as were Pup's.

"I don't want you to be broken if I'm gone. I know and love that you depend on what I give you and what we do, but I don't want you to waste away or fade out onto the street. I don't want you to give up, okay?"

Pup was puzzled back then and in the present as they watched.

"I won't. You've made me better and stronger and happier, and I'm not gonna just—"

"I'm gonna be gone for a week. I told you how it is."

Pup nodded.

"I know."

"You'll get to join me on the next of these trips."

Pup shook their head.

"I trust you, you—"

"You'll come."

The scene faded. The moonlight and the blue and the dog and the ghostly air faded away. Houston was clinging tight to Pup; Asha was shaking her head dozens of times. Lex and Luna were sleeping deep somehow, no doubt brought to this point by the aid of several substances. This had not been the first thing Pup had not understood of late, but it was the first one that let Pup know there was more to be understood.

I HOPE I PASSED THE AUDITION

The heat of the slap. The splash of saliva on her eyes. Houston smiled, anointed and twice blessed. Trent was bearing Daddy's love, and Daddy was so full of love. She looked up into Trent's eyes and showed him, imagining as she did the beauty and majesty of Daddy's wives and the touch of his long-fingered hands upon her and then inside her, the feel of his lips, of teeth upon her, and the tender and the rough and the loving touch that had made her so completely and utterly his. In the Big Room, they didn't care for Trent, but Houston loved him very much. Houston wanted to do the impossible and to make him happy. She reached up with her dextrous tongue to lap some saliva from her face.

"Thank you," she said. "I love you."

He grabbed a nipple and twisted hard; he spat in her face again. The bulge in those leather pants was moving, growing with each act of degradation and violence on the body he'd been entrusted with. Trent loved Daddy, and Trent loved his job, and Houston loved Trent. That's why he laid in with another slap, harder, more impassioned with more backhand in it. She did not flinch but leaned in and treated it as the gift that it was, and it was a gift, a gift from Daddy, which was the very finest kind of gift. A wedding gift? Could it have been a wedding gift? She would look so lovely as a bride! She felt her girlcock strain against the chastity cage at the thought.

"Do you think that I want you, you sick little faggot? Do you think I don't know a fucking boy in a dress when I see one? Getting excited like that, you might as well be calling me a homo like that. Do you think I'm some kind of fucking homo, queerbait?"

The strain at the cage was an ecstasy of its own.

"No, sir, I know a real man when I see one."

The hand on her nipple moved to her throat. He spat on her face again, this time aiming for her nostrils as he choked her.

"Do you? Because it looks like you think I don't like pussy and that I'm going to settle for your dirty, stinking, hairy asshole. Maybe you think I'm going to suck that pathetic cock like one of your leather boys."

She could not say no. She could not shake her head. She was so vulnerable and so compromised in this man's strong, violent hands, hands that served Daddy, hands that squeezed and pinched and punished for Daddy's sake, hands that felt so good on her. Daddy was so good to bring her Trent and Trent's touch, Trent's rage and Trent's love. Each gasp for air was delight, each thrash in his grasp asserting the power that she was under and could not and would not dream to resist.

"I guess you do."

A hard right jab to the gut crumpled her, took more wind from her. It was starting to get hard to breathe; she was starting to hit the brink. Fuck, this might be the day he snuffed her. Maybe he would bring her body back to Daddy and Daddy would use it until she fell apart, until the very structural integrity could not help but yield under the power of his weight and his cock. Fuck, maybe this was the day. Her body, stiff and unresponsive, yielding under Daddy's touch because the time to resist had passed by long, long ago. Fuck. She hoped this would be the day.

"I could kill you right now. Do you not fucking understand? Are you so stupid that you'd just let me choke you to death right here?"

She did not respond; she gasped and let more of the life out of her lungs. He was going to do it. She had fantasized about guys doing it, but this one had the balls and this one had the strength and this one was Daddy's. He had no respect for her body, no respect for her of any kind. He regarded her as something so nasty and wrong and exploitable that he had no qualms at all about murdering such a filthy snuffslut fuckdoll. The only thing that would be bad about dying was that she would never be able to make Daddy happy again, though Daddy would enjoy her body even in death.

Trent tossed her to the bed, made her feel tiny and insignificant and let him exult in tossing her around. Maybe he wouldn't fully snuff her, but he would be able to fully indulge in his violence and perversity. Trent was good at hurting, and part of Houston hungered for that, just as it hungered for death and the cessation of need. Though struggling for breath, she still smiled at him, excited for what was coming next from Trent.

"How do you look at me," he began, hovering just above her, "how do you look at me and fucking smile?"

He loosed two more jabs to her stomach, leaned in and bit her hard on the face, just shy of drawing blood. She could feel him sinking his teeth into her cheek and getting ready to rend and shred a good chunk of it off.

Maybe he would use those teeth and make another precious orifice in her for him to fuck. She had had both him and Daddy in her mouth and in her ass and had lamented that even when Daddy made her the sweetest pussy a woman could ever have, she would not possibly have enough holes.

"How"

—Jab—

"Do"

—Jab—

"You"

—Jab—

"Fucking"

—Was that a rib? Oh, let it be a rib—

"Smile?"

He turned her over, grabbed her by the hair, and threw her over his lap. He let loose a series of spanks, harder and harder. He drew the knife from his belt and struck her time after time after time with the flat of the blade, turning her ass from beige to pink to red, the red darkening again with this series of powerful and sadistic hits painting her different shades with the pain, violence, and intimacy escalating in tandem. He was not harming her worse but actually working to bring some satisfaction. In an odd way, the balance of the situation had shifted, and if Houston had wished to seize it, then she could, but that was not Houston's way.

Houston twitched and trembled with each spank of the knife.

"Cut me open," she cooed. "Make a new hole and fuck it. Cum in my blood and eat my skin. I need you. You're so fucking hot and you're so fucking good to me, Trent."

The spanking with the knife came down harder, shaking and pulsing through her body. He did not turn it and plunge it in or slide it over to take a piece of flesh, though, of course, her words were tempting him, but he spanked harder, focusing on the spots of red that he could start to turn purple, the skin he could paint in his ideal necrotic palette. He exulted in each squeal, each movement, and they drove his cock into something almost pained, rubbing hard and strained against the leather as her cock was against the chastity cage. She was so fucked-up, and there was something starting between them and springing to life, not just him.

"You'd like that, wouldn't you? You'd like it if I covered you with cuts. You'd like if I ripped you up and took your guts out and used your blood for lube to fuck the open chambers of your heart. You like knowing that you could be kept alive only because you're good for one fucking thing. You fucking mess, this is serious. This is life and death. You won't just pop back up fine when I finish. I will leave you bled out, empty, broken. You might wanna be Daddy's wife, but you can't say this shit, you can't tempt me like this."

Trent was tearing up as the spanking escalated harder, tensing and winding up his strikes to let her feel false moments of bodily autonomy but so hungry for the pain and the breakdown and the damage he could cause, so hungry that he broke rhythm. She could make him make a mistake, and her face said she didn't care. She kept talking.

"I want you tempted; I want you hard. I want you to leave nothing left of me but a pool of your cum and satisfaction. I used to think I was scared of death, but no, I was scared that I would never see what it was to feel love. I want to see what love means to you. Is it ripping me up?"

"I don't love!" he screamed. "Daddy says I can't love! Daddy says no! Daddy says I hurt. Daddy says I gotta take you to the brink."

Houston, too, began to cry.

"I love Daddy so fucking much, baby."

Red became purple in his fervor. She tensed and loosened, leaned and moved into the pain dance. He was used to giving out pain, but she was giving herself to it, thorough and eager and so full of generosity. He struck her, and in those strikes, they shared a connection that deepened with every slap, with every wince, and every excited breath. He wanted to split her open in so many ways, and she wanted to let him, and that was no secret between them.

"It's okay," she said breathily, feeling intense and raw and real and sexy as she did. "Anything you need to do is love, and I want it from you so bad. Everything is okay, Trent."

Trent hesitated in his strikes. He sat down on the bed and buried his face in his hands.

"It's not okay. I don't … I'm not supposed to … it's not okay here. It's bad. You should go; I wish you could go and have a life and be safe. You don't want what you think you want."

She crawled to him, wrapping her arms around him.

"You don't have to worry about me. I want whatever is coming. I'm excited and I'm ready. Cassilda and them, they're everything I've ever wanted to be. I want to be one of them. I want to be one of Daddy's wives."

Trent shook his head.

"You don't want that. Might be better if I just killed you right now and spared you that. I don't want Daddy mad, I don't want to disobey, but goddammit, I don't want that for you."

"Lie down," she said.

"Are you telling me what to do?"

She kissed his cheek.

"I'll make it worth your while. You can wreck my ass, and I'll make you cum. You need to relax."

Suddenly, Trent was the one being ordered around.

Suddenly, Trent was the one faced by a wave of sensations. She held down his hands as she guided him to the mattress, then opened her mouth, making him feel not just comfortable but safe having his balls in a vulnerable and compromised place. Trent, who recognized everything as war and power and violence and violation, let himself lie down vanquished and vulnerable and feel something that wasn't pain or the glee of imparting it. He surrendered to tiny tongue shocks, to the warmth and comfort of that mouth that wanted him to have something like peace and something like joy occur.

He hardened to the point of withdrawal and strain and the edges of personal agony. He was hard enough that, from that point, she could mount him. He surrendered to her ass enveloping him and her body bouncing up and down, shuddering with simultaneous pain and joy at the cock underneath her, tight enough that she almost hurt him back with those ministrations. He grabbed on to sweet little pyramidal tits, twisting the nipples with all the sadistic strength he could muster to regain some control, even if it wouldn't and didn't matter at all if he did.

She cried out, let him know he was still hurting her, even if these things were coming together into a single big, broad sensation. She let him feel that satisfaction but didn't take away from him the feeling that he was dangerous. Trent's eyes wandered to the corner of the room. If Houston were paying attention, she would have spotted that they were being observed by a figure so tiny it was barely visible. Daddy was watching, and Daddy approved.

Pup had been gathered up by Daddy's crew and brought to a handsome, bearded gentleman in an Armani suit. There was champagne for the first time in this better-appointed room. Pup did not know what building they were in or how this related to the big room or any other room, but this was the first room Pup had encountered in this wherever that featured not just a bed but also a table on which foods had been laid out. Pup must have been eating but couldn't remember the last time they did. Pup had eaten three times a day, and it was delicious. Daddy was very generous in every way.

"Sit," said the gentleman.

Pup got down on their knees and sat on their feet.

The gentleman scratched Pup's head.

"Would you care for some fruit?"

Pup was not sure if they cared for some fruit but was certain that they were to take the fruit if offered. Pup barked in assent, and the gentleman fed them a strawberry. It felt nice to have fruit, it felt nice to be fed, and it made the gentleman a lot less scary. Daddy was to be trusted, and this was Daddy's friend. Pup did not think anything of the man moving directly behind them, starting to stroke and pinch and knead Pup's ass. This escalated faster than Pup would like; this escalated with no lube and several intense fingers.

The john extended his hand, closing up his fist, moving it around inside of Pup. Pup's asshole was dry, the john only more zealous in his touch as Pup squirmed against it. The suggestion, the pills, the poppers, they were doing nothing. There was not a pleasure to be extracted from this man's hands; they had been used to hurt much more than they'd been used to bring satisfaction to anyone but himself. There was nothing more substantial or powerful in the john's world than his desires, nothing more meaningful than his hungers and fancies.

"Do you want it, little doggie, little bitch in heat?"

No. I don't want this, you sadistic fuck. Please stop. This hurts. You're fucked in the fucking head. Take it out of me. Leave and fix yourself. Leave and don't touch me. I don't want this. You're fucking hurting me. I am not OW *I am not not not ow stop stop stop it hurts, I don't want this, you fucking psycho, take it out of me take it out of me you disgusting fucking* OW! Pup wanted to scream out and beg him to stop, but there was no voice to be found, no access to any kind of insubordination. Pup had to roll with the pain; Pup had to remind themself that Daddy wouldn't let this guy damage something he considered his. They may have been an object, but they were also a possession. Pup still wanted to shout and protest and disengage. It did not come out like that. It twisted in Pup's brain, transforming into the one word Pup least wanted to say. It was Daddy who chose the word, Daddy who prodded Pup with the invisible lightning fingers on pliant brain to shock synapses into the accomplices the monster wanted most. Treason of body, treason of mind, seized by the need for love and unconditional approval.

"Yes."

With his left hand, the man tugged on the leash. He pulled out and turned Pup to face him. His eyes were ablaze with arousal and cruelty alike, a sign that he was just beginning with Pup and that Pup was lucky Daddy wanted to keep everyone in the Big Room alive. Daddy was nice that way. Daddy was so kind and gracious. No harm would come to Pup if Pup just trusted Daddy, even if this man here was getting extremely scary and dangerous looking. Pup waited for the next instruction, not surprised to see the man put his blood- and shit-caked fist in Pup's face.

"You're a fucking dog; you know what to do."

Pup took a deep breath and thought of Daddy's love, Daddy's power, Daddy's wrath, though surely Daddy had to be kind. If Daddy were not kind, he would not keep poor bereaved Pup as a doggie, adored and pampered and given all that they could ever want. The john scared Pup, but Daddy in his infinite wisdom surely put this man here as a test of faith in how much Daddy knew what was best. This faith should have been unwavering, and Pup felt bad for feeling these pangs of alien doubt, pangs that belonged outside of this place for love and sex and sanctity.

Pup did what a dog was to do. It tasted like ice cream. Maybe it was ice cream. No, that couldn't be. Maybe, somehow, they'd been taught that shit and blood caked on a pervert's fist would taste like ice cream. Daddy would not do such a thing. It tasted like ice cream. It would be the work of a cruel omnipresence and not a loving benefactor to make such a claim. Pup lapped and kissed and gulped off the clumps of their body, their excrement left on that hand and felt a throb between their legs as they did so.

"Thank you," said Pup.

The john slapped Pup across the face hard. Pup did not like it. Pup liked it a lot. This didn't seem right. Something in Pup pushed up against these thoughts, some neglected strength. There were things in there that had not come there naturally. This situation was in fact scary. Pup did not like the slapping. Pup did not like to be handled like this. Pup did not like to be no Pup liked Pup liked Pup liked Pup did not like that there was no escape.

A swell of pain and heat came through Pup. It came quick, it came hard and sudden, and it filled Pup's body far more than the cock of the stranger using them as hard as they could. Whatever this was, was not drugs, was not abuse, was not the overpowering mental illness and despair. This was something else altogether, a force that would do its whim and have its way no matter how hard anyone dared struggle against it. It was coming on strong and hard and fast, and Pup could feel that again they were but a plaything.

"Something, something's wrong," said Pup, face sweating and agonized.

Pup's legs wobbled, crunching, cracking, tearing, lengthening. Their arms extended, pulsing with muscle, elongating and reforging, putting meat and muscle and sinew on elongated, transforming bones. What once were fingertips were now long, razors, bones, rippers, organic shears unlike any that he had seen in nature. There was an imposing power to this figure Pup was becoming, but it was more upsetting that this body was becoming something entirely inhuman, breaking down everything that it was.

The john panicked at the snapping of bones that he heard. The little femboy he'd been fucking was shattering and reconfiguring, turning into another entity entirely, something that shouldn't have, couldn't have been real. It was obvious and yet impossible what the body was becoming, and that was a thing of mortal terror, but the excruciating pain that followed as the asshole he was fucking reshaped and clenched, with musculature and power far exceeding that of any creature you should have your dick inside, squeezing, ravaging, and positively wrecking the cock. Vise grip. Guillotine. The fragile human meat wasn't standing a chance. Flesh and muscle alike was being cut, squished, and utterly wrecked.

Stuck. He was stuck. He attempted to pull out of Pup, but the shifting, changing furry body was strong, tightening still, seizing and squeezing and taking it in. He could feel the sharp pain of burst blood vessels. Pup was reconfiguring, growing, but the pain and the pressure were consistent, and the limp, bleeding, dislocated member inside wasn't going anywhere. This hot little piece of ass was becoming something more canine than human.

Pup's face contorted, elongated as their body had. Mouth became snout, teeth pushed free, past evolution, past humanity and into the last eldritch reaches of a cold, unfeeling food chain. A long predator's snout adorned and equipped with sixty bony caltrops where thirty-two teeth once had been was a fine rebuttal to the project of civilization. A long, ravenous, drooling canine head turned to face a horrified and shattered man trying to extricate his unmade meat and, with a single chomp and a rapid tear, parted the tenuous link between skull and physiognomy, leaving a bleeding, shrieking mess which Pup eagerly gulped down.

Pup stood up, seven and a half feet high, covered in fur, sleek legs elongated into limbs not unlike those of a coyote, arms and furred hands now ending in claws like steak knives at the end of each finger. Those arms were gangly, imprecise, but deadly, knuckles threatening to drag on the ground like an ape's. Pup led with those knuckles, hominid and wolf as one, bounding up the stairs to find two of the gangbang crew had come to check out the commotion.

One swipe, one wicked gash so deep you could fuck it. The person in Pup, now barely there, suggested quietly not to do so, and Pup relented only because tearing his throat out and eating it would serve the hunger better. The other reached for his taser but was stopped by Pup grabbing his arm, yanking it clean out of the socket as if this gruff old biker was only a Ken doll in the hands of a sadistic child. A snap of bone, a spray of blood. A screaming dirtbag, dead on the floor.

Daddy's laughter. Daddy's face. Then sleep. Pup's eyes blinked open a split second, found NotMillie curled up nearby. The dead dog had some fur.

GIRLS' NIGHT

Dana was having margaritas after work, hanging out with a couple of girlfriends that she hadn't been great at keeping in touch with. She had been texting Christian some memes she'd found cute, lamenting from time to time that she would have rather stayed home tonight. It would have felt better if she'd chosen to stay home, catch up on heartbreaking, justice-forward documentaries instead of having to witness her thirsty friends disparaging other friends that she was fairly certain she would never hear from as long as she lived and then shit-talking their spouses, most of whom she had not even met. Were she to calculate the value of the gossip she was accumulating, she was fairly sure it wouldn't buy her anything at the Taco Bell drive-through. These were her friends, and she didn't want to be thinking or talking about them like this, but they were making it tough not to.

"And then just falls asleep," said Becca at the tail end of something. "Three pumps and he acts like he's doing me a favor, you know? That bullshit was supposed to go out with my dad's generation."

"Yeah," said Other Becca, "I hate that you're having

boomer sex. But fuck, maybe I'm having boomer sex, you know? Like, I don't know how much I really like my husband."

"Then get a divorce," said Elsa. "You don't have to be miserable."

Other Becca stirred her drink listlessly.

"I don't think I want to get a divorce. I think it just needs to be better. Maybe he needs to see a therapist, or I need to see a therapist, or we both need to see a therapist."

The genuine needs of her friends felt more acute suddenly, got some meat on their bones. Dana had hoped she would actually feel some connection to these people she had known and supported and gotten support from for as long as she had. They had been there when she was doubting Christian's fidelity, before he started taking his antidepressants. She had gotten a lot from nights like this and found them invaluable back then, so she was feeling a bit callous for caring less and wishing herself out of what had been meaningful friendships with meaningful people who had wanted much more from life than they had gotten.

"I think that you probably should see someone. I remember how it was with Christian after his dad died. He was so distant, and he was out at bars and going to the movies alone. I'm not an idiot. I thought some shit was going down, right? But he wasn't doing healthy grief and owning his shit. That was it. We're, like, twice a week now, and it's good."

"Yeah," said Becca, "but what if you want to do it more than twice a week?"

"Then you shouldn't have gotten married, bitch," said Morgan, which brought about loud peals of cleansing laughter, even though it was more harsh than funny.

Nonetheless, this was a thing the conversation and

everyone in it needed a lot. Variants of light and dark and heft and levity were what made these nights out together so crucial in the past. Terminally single and eagerly slutty, Morgan was, like most people who get laid all the time, pretty good at code switching, and this was a gift.

"I wanna fuck the man I married," said Becca. "I married him because he was a guy I desired. It feels almost pervy to desire your husband, but I'm there. I want more than for him to get on top and cum and roll over and sleep."

"Do you tell him?" Morgan asked.

It didn't take a rocket scientist to figure out what the reply would be. None of them really communicated that well with their husbands. Christian was inconsistent in his affection and attention; Christian was somewhere else a lot, not literally like it used to be but inside. The antidepressants had made a difference, but still there were occasions when he was right there and words shouted and echoed down a great, dark empty hallway. Dana didn't want to be alone, even if she was in fact frequently alone. She didn't tell Christian half of what she wanted to, so there was no way Becca told her husband anything like that.

Becca shrugged. "Should I? I'm happy enough, I think. I could just make him think I'm ungrateful or make him even worse if I open my mouth about it. I should just get a Hitachi and give myself what I'm not getting."

"Or you could try and make shit better," said Elsa. "We gotta stand up for what we want out of relationships."

Dana noticed the strong, handsome, bald gentleman at the bar again. She had noticed him when they came in, she had continued to notice him at several other points in the conversation, and his glances back indicated that he had probably noticed her. His black tank top made him look sleek and swole, underdressed for the bar but belonging there nonetheless. He'd gone through an order of steak tartare, nursed a martini, then ordered a second, letting it breathe and letting it last. He was handsome and powerful and clearly had taste, and he was consistently glancing over at her. She didn't see the look on his face on Christian's very often.

"The guy at the bar's cute," said Morgan with a wry smile.

"He is," said Becca. "If I were single, I'd fucking hit that."

"I'm married and I'd fucking hit that," said Elsa. "The man's hot, and he's looking at Dana like a dog looks at a roast on the counter."

"She ain't wrong," said Morgan, putting a hand on Dana's thigh. "He seems interested. You should talk to him."

Dana laughed.

"The fuck is wrong with you people? Do you think I'm going to choose to cheat on my husband just because some hot guy at a bar is giving me the opportunity? I don't need to take every chance I can get to get laid. I'm not a teenage boy."

"He's so hot," said Elsa. "Do you not see how hot that guy is? If you don't do it, I'm gonna. I told you I'd fucking hit that."

"Then you should," said Dana. "You should fucking hit that since it's so easy."

A waitress approached from the bar with a whiskey sour.

"The gentleman at the bar bought you this," she said to Dana, "but I'd understand if you—"

"It's fine," said Dana, smiling at the waitress.

"Cool," said the waitress, taking her leave.

"Well now you gotta," said Other Becca, who'd been

pretty quiet.

Dana raised the glass to the man at the bar. The bald, handsome gentleman raised his in return but did not make a move to approach. She took a sip. The whiskey sour was nice, made with a solid mid-shelf bourbon that showed a modicum of personal taste. This was a simple drink but ordered by a man with a certain amount of class, putting in just enough effort to let her know that he cared about her experience. It was nice that someone cared about her experience. She felt a tinge of remorse over her marriage, a kinship with the other bad marriages around her.

So, she could find her way home to a husband who was not all the way there, spending time in a world that was not hers and she would never be invited into. She could sit and drink with them, or she could say hello and maybe have a good time with a man who was willing to pay her some attention. Would it really hurt to have someone pay attention to her like that? She stood up and walked toward the prospect of being seen and known and desired. Something about him made her nervous, but those nerves made her excited.

"Hi," she said to the bald, muscular gentleman, "thank you for the drink."

The man turned to her, fixed, intense, a magnetic pulse of attention catching her and absorbing her.

"Thank you for making the bar a brighter, lovelier place. The price of a drink is a pittance in comparison."

She smiled. The line wasn't great, but there was a sincerity and longing behind it that she appreciated. This man laid bare the longing and showed himself, a master, a slave, a disciple of it. In other circumstances, it would frighten her to be wanted so much, a liability transforming oh so quickly into an outright threat. She leaned into this thirst and discomfort because they were becoming rarer things in her life. It was not common to feel like someone wanted her so much that they might do something crazy.

"I think you should know that I'm married."

The man did not look away. His attention did not for a moment waver or soften. He remained intent on locking her in place and in this context. He remained intent on where he was and what they were speaking of and did not give so much as a flinch in response. Looking at him, it seemed as if this was a man who had never flinched or backed away from anything in his life and did not plan to start here.

"I think you should know, then, that I absolutely do not give a shit. What you have told me is worse than useless to me because it could get in the way of me pinning you down and using you until we are both aching and sore and very, very spent. Your marital status does not concern me because I want you and I am not in the habit of letting men I do not know or care about get in the way of me doing whatever I fucking please."

She was taken aback somewhat. He was bold, even for a guy in a downtown bar. He was sure of himself and sure of her, and he would have been her worst nightmare if she didn't want everything he was offering her.

"How do you know it doesn't matter to me? How do you know that I don't love my husband?"

He shrugged.

"It's not that I don't know. It's that I don't care. It matters how much you care that you love your husband, but there's little I can do to change that beyond offer you a good time, which is what I am doing. It is your decision whether you take that offer or not. But I think you're going to take it."

The women at the table were laughing into their hands. They could have intervened and helped her stand her ground, or they could have called her a cab and sent her home, but none of them did because they would probably have been tempted to do the same and could not help but applaud her bravery in the circumstances. There was no more reason to turn back, no reason to doubt.

"My name is Dana," she said to him, "and I want you to show me a good time."

"I'm Trent," he replied, "and I will."

It took two of Daddy's gangbang crew under the supervision of their leader to get the great hairy thing down the stairs. Long-limbed, muscular, an ogre with the face and snout of some genetic throwback to a wolf or dog. There was a collective shudder running through the room. Asha, Luna, and Lex were as scared as one another for once. The fog of lust and confusion had been parted completely with the new realization that this monster existed and was being brought to them, brought perhaps to cause them harm. It looked deadly, even in its state of unconscious repose. It looked more ferocious and twisted than anything in nature should look and capable of so much more if provoked.

"What the fuck is that?" Lex asked. "I need you to get that out of here. We don't want it."

"Well," said the head of the crew, "your little friend here took out one of Daddy's best customers and took out two of the crew. Daddy thinks it might be fun to start over, get some new fresh meat in here. Most of the time, this thing's gonna be harmless, but not tonight, no fucking sir. This FUCKING THING'S GONNA FUCK!"

The head of the crew laughed his raw, half-gone nitrous laugh.

"It's gonna fuck you in the fucking guts. It's gonna tear you open and play with your insides. Your little friend is a monster. Not like Trent, not like me, not like Daddy, naw, this here's a real monster, motherfuckin' cock-suckin' werewolf. Never thought a werewolf could take dick like this one, but shit, werewolf's got some fine-ass bussy and a fine-ass mouth. Big ole claws, though, big ole teeth."

"You can fuckin' say that again," said the other guy from the crew. "Left a big ole mess. Lucky Daddy could clean it up and get this thing to sleep. Maybe it'll sleep through the day and the night, but I wouldn't count on it."

"Might not even turn back to normal," said the head of the crew. "Don't know if werewolves are like that. Might wake up and eat you straight away. You should pray that this werewolf just wakes up and eats ya. Ripped Chester up good. Ripped Norm up good. Thing kills good as it fucks. Better than me."

"Don't take much to fuck better than you," Lex spat.

The two dropped the unconscious wolf creature on the mattress. The leader of the crew turned around and took Lex's throat in his hand, then leaned in close, headbutting him hard, so hard it nearly knocked Lex out, so hard it gave him a nosebleed. Lex was fuzzy, head covered in blood, getting stumbly from the force and suddenness of the attack. For some reason, the crew leader gave out another high-pitched nitrous cackle.

"You know firsthand don't nobody fuck like I do! I'm the fuckmaster! I'm a goddamn cock coach, and you respect my fucking rank, even if it don't matter none because you're gonna die, which ya are, you know, you're gonna die."

"It's fake," said Lex, pressing a hand against his

head. "This is a prop. It's just something to fuck with our heads."

"It ain't like that," said the other gangbang boy. "This is the real McCoy. Actual honest-to-god lycanthrope. Maybe you're too stupid to know one when you see one, but Daddy ain't, and Daddy says that was a werewolf."

"Oh," said Asha softly, "I shoulda known Pup was different."

"That thing ain't Pup!" Lex shouted back. "They're fuckin' with us."

"We ain't fuckin' with you," said the leader, smiling a methed-out smile. "But this fucker's gonna fuck with you, gonna fuck with your guts because it's a giant razor-clawed, wolf-jawed guts-fucker! Any of you want a taste of this here dick before this monstrosity sends you onto Hell, you oughta, ya know. You oughta get you a taste of heaven before hell comes round."

"You should take him up," said the gangbang boy, "because he can show you again how a cockmaster does it. Daddy don't have time to touch you. Daddy doesn't love you anymore."

"Maybe Daddy never loved us," said Asha, "maybe we were wrong and now we're going to pay."

Luna stood up.

"What the fuck, Asha? You can't possibly think that! He's provided for us and given us a home. You certainly do enough of his fucking drugs, Asha. I don't know what's going on here, but Daddy's going to fix whatever it is."

Asha laughed as loud and full-throated as the crew leader did, with the same degree of derision.

"You're a dumb cunt, Luna. Always were. Always have to look on the bright side. I know you don't believe that because you know we're fucked. You know how I know? Daddy has stopped hiding everything from us. He no longer has to bother. Daddy is a monster, and

Pup is a monster too. There's so little life left to enjoy, and we're not going to enjoy it."

"She's right," said the gangbang boy. "If Daddy lets you know what he's done, then it's too late."

"You're being a bitch, Asha."

Asha slid her shorts down, lay back on the mattress, and beckoned the leader of the crew over.

"Let's see how a cockmaster does it. It's been a while since I've been any good to Daddy."

Lex's jaw dropped.

"What the fuck, Asha?"

Asha shrugged. Her eyes were still as bright and far off and inscrutable, still looking through the ketamine haze. Junkie. Whore. Seer. She was a bit more of the woman who'd come into this, and that wasn't a great endorsement for her state of mind. Lex saw that this woman who he had come to get close to was surrendering to every possible thing she could surrender to. Asha knew things somehow, and Lex would prefer to have been far away from that knowledge or for that knowledge to be untrue.

The leader shoved casually past Lex, unzipped his pants, and started working his dick.

"That's it, honey," said Asha, less herself, or more herself, a tone that Lex had not heard for ages. "You deserve this. You deserve this pussy. You have served Daddy so well."

"Asha!" Lex shouted, "Don't fucking touch him."

The crew leader didn't need Asha's help getting hard enough to get inside her. Maybe her legs and cunt were hairier than he usually preferred, and he had forgotten to bathe her the previous day due to all the other excitement, but he saw what he wanted and he got on top, body weight moving at a fevered, frenetic, animal hump that was artless but was hitting the right places. He was on her; he was deep; hairy, mottled, pasty old ass on display as he had his way with the slender young thing that had given up so much on life in that moment. They had been used by him but usually as a matter of obligation, not a choice, not something so strange and inappropriate for the moment.

Lex wanted to shove the guy off of Asha, wanted to talk some sense into her, but there were two more of those clowns around, and at his strongest, he would likely not have been able to take them out. He did not know when and how much he was eating, how often he actually had been lifting the weights by the mattress, and if the T was coursing through him right. Lex wanted to shake Asha out of this and find some way to survive it, but she was rolling and scratching the leader's back, not wincing as he spat in her face. He thought of his feelings for Asha, made ugly as they could be by the surges of doubt and contempt and by the veneer of love for Daddy.

One of the men from the crew approached Lex, putting an arm around his waist. Lex placed a hand on the gangbang boy's.

"Just this," said Lex, actually appreciating the warmth.

"Okay," said the gangbang boy. It was a bit of a surprise.

"Thanks," said Lex.

"You know," said the gangbang boy, "I really do like fucking you."

"Thanks."

Asha's eyes, distant as usual, were locked onto the leader's, gaze clamping tight as her cunt and legs were, and they were indeed clamping tight. She clung to him for the little bit of life she could squeeze from the moment, scraped nails hard, and found he was indeed a master of his cock, as obnoxious as it might have been to call himself that. She came quickly the first time; she came and she rode the orgasm at length, letting it fade so she could work toward another one and she could get as much as she could from what could have been the last good thing, bad as the last good thing was, wrong as the last good thing was. The last good thing didn't have to be good all the way, though, because it would be the last.

She squeezed him and his cock and his body tight, proximity to something that would make it through the night and a reminder that there was still something in her to celebrate and indulge. She rose to meet him and fell to rise to meet him again, body pleading another long, intense orgasm from her as Lex relaxed into the arms of the gangbang boy.

Luna rose and walked to them, her body joining them, mutely enjoying the feel of another as Asha played out the fucked-up and confused pantomime of a person reduced to an object, then told that their time even as an object was at an end. Bodies again. Bodies were the only answer. In the dread of all of it, in the confusion of a tissue paper life, they found bodies. Fevered, wholesome, warm, right, wrong, there were bodies and there was humanity. As little as that throng had in common and as sick as they might have been from the condition of being that thing, that fragile thing, that bloody, brainsick, dying thing, they got to feel each other.

The other gangbang boy joined in the chaste embrace as Asha milked all she could from the leader, who spent himself just as she got into her third, knee-shaking orgasm, and then pressed him close enough that even he must have felt like something precious and good and important; beyond his member, beyond his ego, and beyond his associations, he was something precious and important and good, and he was making her happy in even this absurd display.

She met his eyes again, and it could have been a plea, but instead, it was connection.

"Do you think he'll let you remember me?" she whispered.

"Fuck you," said the leader. "You gotta ruin everything every time you open your damn whore mouth?"

"Yeah," said Asha, "I do. You came in me, and you won't even remember me. Go back to whatever the fuck you're doing and let me wait for the grave."

The leader, the cockmaster, trudged off in shame alongside the other two gangbang boys.

The wolfish shape was twitching on the mattress, letting out tiny canine yips, a dog in its sleep, maybe dreaming of chasing rabbits or the promise of more flesh in those powerful jaws. The three watched, frightened. By the time Lex could think to pursue them and maybe jump them before they got the door to wherever they were open, the men had come and gone, leaving them to this monstrosity before them, a creature they all, in various ways, had started to trust and like. Luna, Lex, and Asha were left to each other's company and each other's pain and each other's loneliness and each other's sudden realization that they had been living in a fog of death and misuse and slavery, a life in which they exchanged all autonomy for moments of satisfied craving. They had traded away all their chances and now had only each other to wait out the end of their lives with, at the claws of someone they were starting to trust and care for.

It took time, but the figure on the floor got smaller, lost the fur, and turned back into someone they recognized. It was clearly daylight now, and the transformation wouldn't come again until nightfall, if that was how it worked. Pup roused and looked at the startled and broken people around them.

"I was somewhere else. Someone or something else was thinking for me. I could hear some things, couldn't see much, but someone else was running my body, and they were big and they were fierce, and I was pretty sure nothing could stop them. I felt less like a person than an animal, not something bad or cruel but something that had stuff to do that people would find cruel and wouldn't understand. I only saw those men and what they'd done and how they were going to hurt more, and I felt that even if I could have stopped the killing, I wouldn't have. I don't know if, when I become that thing again, I'll know you guys from them at all. You'll be people, and I'll be something completely inhuman."

Asha laughed, and it cut.

"We're barely people now, Pup. We're things, discarded things left to die. I don't know if I was all that good at bein' a person. I think I'd rather be like that. How did you get to be like that?"

Pup sighed, trying to sort everything out, trying to figure out what to say. If they were in danger and could die, what they said could be anything.

"There was a woman I loved. She had me as her partner, her sub, her Puppy. She would vanish for a few days a month, had business to do, and I'd be lonely, but I let myself accept it, and she was adamant that I couldn't be part of that. Until last month right before she disappeared, she bit me, and it broke the skin. I didn't know what that meant, if anything. I didn't think it was important. I couldn't have known what she was giving me. She seemed to know that things were going to get bad, and I think she wanted me to survive and be strong like she was. I think she was too strong, and when she bit me, she made me strong as she was. When it's night, whenever night is, I feel like I'll be that thing again because she bit me and she finally broke the skin."

Lex laughed, shook his head.

"Shit, Pup, this place has made us so fucking crazy; you know that? I have no idea what the fuck you're talking about."

Luna stroked Lex's shoulder.

"Maybe you don't, but you know, it doesn't make less sense than a lot of things we've seen here. I think maybe Pup was given a gift. Maybe if Pup's a werewolf, then they can stand up to Daddy. They can take down all them boys in the gangbang crew, and they can take down the brides and then Daddy. That thing Pup turned into was real big. Didn't look like there was much that could stop it, 'cept for if Daddy told them to go to sleep."

"Daddy's as strong as Daddy wishes to be. He's big as he wishes to be. Pup couldn't take out Daddy alone, and if we're just us, then it doesn't matter if Pup is strong enough to take out Daddy. There might be a way, though. Pup's partner gave them that strength with the bite, and Pup got strong enough to fight back against that john and the gangbang crew. I want that strength."

Pup winced.

"I don't know what it is, I don't know how to make sense of it, and I don't even know if it'll work."

Luna clutched Pup tight to her chest, kissed Pup's head, let Pup breathe. Luna was good at letting people breathe. Luna was good.

"The worst that happens is just another bite mark. After Daddy and Daddy's wives, another bite is us getting off easy, even if you've gotta break the skin."

Pup nodded, then sank teeth into Luna's shoulder, feeling a tinge of excitement as they gripped at that pliant and delightful flesh, as it needed and gave way as they fought against the barriers of smooth skin, and even in the horror, even in the hopelessness, there was a tiny tinge of giddy thrill, organic, not reminiscent of the eldritch pheromone nonsense Daddy's control had been wafting in but instead the joy of knowing they didn't need to give in and they didn't need to stop, that maybe nothing could hold them back again.

There was no discernible place this feeling came from, not really, and no way beyond instinct of knowing if or how any of it could work. What was clear, though little else was, was that the bite was something wholly theirs and Daddy could not take it away. A marked, ecstatic Luna backed off and let Asha, then Lex come forth and engage in the ritual. They focused on pain and on the wolf, on freedom, on how they could learn to move and fight as one, and on the end of the monster that kept them prisoner, who would not give them a second chance to get out.

The four lay together on Pup's mattress, pressed against one another and waiting. As they did, something began to happen. Sure as the ocean itself could, they could feel it: the moon approaching, the Earth drawing close to the mother of tides, and change. As they lay waiting, each could tell deeply, in their wearied bones, misused flesh, and challenged blood, that the Full Moon was on its way and, with it, a chance, even a fragment, a shadow, a ghost of a chance that they could once again see daylight. There had been so little for them out there before, but whatever there was, was better than this. They did not talk, they did not weep, they did not fuck, but they held each other and let the moon come forth.

"Yes," said Millie's voice in Pup's ear, now present in the real world instead of the half dream where they'd met, "you've shared the gift, and you might just make it out of this alive."

Though in Daddy's realm, there was no sign of sun or moon, they were inevitable. Sure enough, the moon would come, and it did. Their bodies began the change. Though Luna shrieked and bent and nearly broke and her flesh and muscles churned, though Lex's arms rippled with new power that shattered and repaired his bones all at once, though Asha stretched into impossible, unmade, remade, coyote lean power that her body had not been made to bear, though their pain was excruciating, it was short lived. When all the reshaping, when all the snapping and mending and shifting had ended, they had become a great round wolfmother, a fierce, strong, dark-grey brute, and a fast, wiry beast still bearing her ever-haunted eyes; and Pup, powerful, bigger, hungrier, a better Pup, an ever-ready Pup. The sacrament was made, the moon rose, and they stood together, ready to function, ready to fight, ready to kill and seek freedom as one.

SACRIFICE

Christian woke up from dozing on the couch. He felt movement, heard a car park and a key turning in the door. Dana must have been back from her night out with the girls. Good for Dana. He was glad she'd stayed out late. He really wanted her to be happy, but he could never figure out what he could do to make that so. He had his own life, secret, somewhat, and separate for certain, and he hoped that hers could be as enriching and promising for her, even though he was likely the thing she needed to escape from. He wanted to feel bad about that, and he did, but he could not muster the energy to really do so. It was good that she'd stayed out late.

It wasn't Dana who walked in. It was three guys, one of them a fit, lean Black guy in a tank top with plenty of muscles, another an older, rounder dude in an open Hawaiian shirt. The third he'd seen around but could not remember his name, though he could certainly tell from his eyes and his wiry, twitchy form that he did not want him in his house and his presence brought ill omen and something worse. Christian did not know what was next and did not relish the thought of it.

"What are you guys doing here?" Christian asked as if a lack of invitation or some element of self-consciousness would be enough to give them pause and prevent that thing they had come here uninvited to do. The leader replied with a derisive snort.

"Shit, man. I been told that you ain't serious, but I don't think they really got at how much of a serious man you ain't. You went lookin' for Daddy like a goddamn moron. Seemed like maybe you thought you weren't gonna find him."

"I was looking for a friend."

The crew laughed again together. Christian wondered if he was going to die.

"Oh, well, why didn't you say so?" said the leader. "Get me a beer and maybe we can be friends."

"Yeah," said Christian, "okay."

Christian was sure as hell not going to not get this guy a beer. He went into the kitchen, immediately telling himself that there was no way he was going to be able to hit the back door or crawl out the window. Wouldn't do much good to pull a knife from out the knife block or to dial the cops. What could potentially work as well as anything could be expected to work was getting this guy a beer and hoping that when the beer was done, this man and his associates would not feel like killing him. He brought the guy a beer.

The leader smiled as he took the beer.

"See, handsome, I told you we could be friends. We're friends now. You understand?"

Christian gulped hard.

"Yeah," Christian said, "we're friends."

The crew all laughed. Christian was certain that he shouldn't laugh along. He was sure he could end up dead if he played a single beat of this meeting wrong and not so sure he could come out alive if he did everything right. He was worried that maybe Dana could walk in and end up getting hurt.

"My wife …"

"My wife," echoed back the scumbag in the Hawaiian shirt, doing his best Borat, which was not very good.

The crew laughed and Christian laughed politely along with them.

"Look, man," said the leader, "your wife is okay, but if you look for Daddy, you're gonna find him. Make your peace with finding Daddy and everyone's gonna be friends. I usually don't get sent to talk to folks calmly, but I been told to gather you up and take you to everyone you wanna see. You're lucky. So how about a fucking thank you, okay?"

Christian nodded.

"Thank you."

The leader finished his beer and pulled a blindfold from his pocket.

"Gonna need you to put this on."

Christian had visions of snuff, visions of ditch-bound death. He was at the mercy of these unstable men who were probably going to rape him as a joyless, howling afterthought. They could do it, they would do it, and there was little they wouldn't be capable of doing to him. He put the blindfold on and, behind it, watched a procession of tortures inflicted upon him, which finally culminated in the release of death.

He was surprised to find that, when the car stopped, they did not immediately get to work on him but instead led him inside a building that smelled of sex and decay. They led him further in a bit before removing his blindfold to reveal that his wife was already at this barely distinguishable place, albeit not a whole lot like herself. The guys who had kidnapped him had kidnapped her first.

Dana was aglow with joy, with awe at something she was looking at somewhere far off from this room full of armed reprobates and her panicking husband. He wanted to shake her hard until she was outside of wherever and then to extricate her from all of this and to live and be safe and reconcile the differences and make peace with both her and himself. He did not like that wide-eyed and ecstatic expression and all that it implied. She may have been subject to some kind of revelation, but he had not, and that was the last thing he wanted at this place and time. They could go and things could be the way they were, if it were possible for them to go, if it were possible for things to be the way they were. They likely weren't going to let her leave with him.

"I'm sorry," he said, starting to sob. "I didn't mean for this to come down on you and to hurt you so bad. I was just trying to …"

She shook her head.

"It's okay, Christian," she said. "I know who you are and what you're up to and where you go, and it's okay. I love you for who you are, and you don't have to hide anything now. I don't have to hide anything. We can stand before each other as we are and be okay here. You're fine, Christian. We're fine."

The leader moved closer to her, pulling out the knife at his side and stabbing her in the stomach. It happened in an instant, the blood gushing, the laughter from Dana, the blue-haired woman gasping in fear and then in delight, the strange man gathering her up in his arms and kissing her, then resting his head on her shoulder as the second of the crew approached and then plunged the knife into her side. More blood, more squeals and peals of laughter. The third offered Christian his knife as he looked on, watching more of his wife's life splatter out into the bucket beneath her, stain the dress. They could have gathered this more efficiently, but that wasn't the point—the pain was the point; the knife was the point.

"I'm not going to stab her," Christian said to the

gangbang boy. "She's my wife. I can't do this to her. I promise I won't—"

"Naw," said the gangbang boy, "it ain't like that. You're in this now. And you could die, and that would be fine; but naw, you're gonna take that knife, and you're gonna look her in the eyes, and you're gonna kill her."

Dana looked at him, gentle laughter on her lips, stab wounds all over her body. There was no saving her. There was no finding the woman that had been there, and there was no surviving this without doing exactly as they said. They parted as he approached, his part of this so much more meaningful than theirs. He looked her in the eyes as he was expected to, took the knife and did as he was expected to. He loved her, he would miss her, he could save her, but she was a price he would pay for living his truth. His hand was just another hand stabbing her, his knife just another knife claiming more of her life for purposes he did not even need explained to him.

She might have been dead the last couple times he stabbed her. It didn't matter if she was. They were still going, and so, too, was he. This body was held up only by the force of another knife trying to extract more from her, trying to cut and take and drain her out into this bucket. There was a cooing, moaning sound in the background as, on the bed, the woman with blue hair watched. She was licking her lips, her hands tented together as if in both anticipation and in prayer.

Christian carried on, smashing pinata, poking holes in the bloodbag that had once been the most important person in his life. He was wasting some, he was sure, sticky red spray covering him almost completely, though most of it still ran down into that bucket, which was filling with as much of the ten pints of her as could be extracted. He stopped when he felt there was nothing left of her.

THE CHASE

"We are chasing fat rabbits," NotMillie explained.

They were on all fours as they ran the woods at night. There were dogs at their back, faint though they were, shadows of dogs, echoes of dogs, thoughts of dogs. A forest alight with eyes, a night alight with forest. NotMillie had skin on her, patchy though it was; NotMillie was looking like Millie and they were chasing fat rabbits, that was all. Pup wore the face of Pup, the body of Pup, though they knew their real one was something else, something big and powerful, indomitable and different. Pup's skin here was slick with blood.

"There's blood on me," said Pup. "I'm sticky with blood."

"We are chasing fat rabbits," NotMillie insisted. "We chase prey. They are running the long night; they are waiting in the dark for us and for the people. Some people have to serve themselves; they must be dog."

"Are you her? How do we do this?"

Innumerable spectral hounds of all sizes, yipping, barking, leaping with excitement. There was gore, there was death, there was horror, but these dogs, these dogs were playing. It was as NotMillie said; they were chasing fat rabbits somewhere out there, even if, perhaps, those rabbits walked and thought and talked and bled and died like men. Prehistoric trees, bent and ancient and altogether wrong, bearing spined and pulsing fruits; a thing in the sky that might have been a pterodactyl screeched.

"I am not. I am Millie; I am dog," said NotMillie. "She is among them, at your back, gone, not gone, hunting. We must hunt."

"All I want is to escape. I want these people to escape too. They don't deserve this."

Millie let out an annoyed dog huff.

"Don't deserve is what the Takers do. There might be justice, but there is none where they want, none under their dominion. They are not people; they do not wish for the Earth to be a place of comfort."

Pup had fought and killed and would fight and kill some more. When the woods were gone and the waking world returned, if Pup lived, Pup would live with gore on their hands and meat on their breath and innumerable questions as well as several truths they could not want, and yet Pup leapt and ran and made their way through these old secret growths wherever they might have been in hopes of seeing that world once more and learning to live with and without that burden. Or were they chasing fat rabbits?

"What is Daddy?"

"Erlkonig, Face Beneath. Not that but of that."

Pup had heard none of these phrases before. The dog was not telling them anything they could use.

"I don't know what you're saying."

Millie gave another irate huff.

"I am dog. Dog does not speak; they listen, they understand. Hopefully, you'll get there someday."

"Someday? What do you mean someday? I need help now."

"You have help. You might just make it out of this

alive. Lenore made you part of the pack, and the pack is behind you, pack is with you."

Pup looked around at lush, green infinity, remembering that outside there was only grey concrete and prison, that the body, driven by the wolf or whatever it was, was fighting something they didn't understand and had only the aid of the others that had been prisoners. Those prisoners had given warmth and time and love, though those prisoners now gave strength and purpose. Warmth and time and love were good, but they would need more than love.

Stench of rot. Smell of hot blood. Stench of bad man. Stink of traitor. Stink of rotten meat and pain and suffering. The sounds of a weeping and a screaming man. The pack followed sharp ears and noses, unable to trust their eyes in this building, for even before the eyes of a pack of wolves, the hallway was still pitch-black, so much so that there were no shapes or landmarks or patterns to recognize. They did not need those. They did not even need to know what guided them or why they had taken on the guise, what lineage or connection they now bore. These things were never important to packs of wolves and dogs, and they would not start mattering.

A towering shadow loomed over the room, perhaps already there. Daddy rose from seemingly nowhere, turned, spat one last gout of blood into Houston's mouth, then seemed to vanish altogether, whether becoming a cloud of mist or becoming tiny enough to slip under the door.

Trent watched in horror as the four creatures came bounding into the room, hairy, long-limbed, lupine bodies full of power, yellow bestial eyes aglow with well-earned wrath. The gangbang crew turned around, Dana's corpse at their feet, knives drawn, and still horrified of what was coming at them. No matter how strong that horror was, however, it was not as strong as the loyalty and fear of Daddy they'd been instilled with. The three gangbang boys went forth to die against the impossible. Christian cradled his dead wife in his arms. Houston swallowed blood and led out moans that could easily have passed for sexual.

The crew surged forward uselessly, tossed backwards by a single long, dismissive swipe that cleaved across all three torsos. Though epitome of ribcage, though devil of starvation, though trappings of want still showed on her body, Asha had the strength in the impossible dirk-clawed arms to anoint the three men effortlessly with the blessing of a wide new orifice. They had taken from the starve-priest and the starve-priest in turn took from them. The wolves could make bigger, more vulgar displays of gore come to pass, but this, this was enough to kill three men in one terrible blow.

Trent stared into the wide-open jaws of ravenous, fanged, drooling death. He knew all of his strength couldn't cut through the hide, couldn't stab the canine ogre before him, could barely nick it if he put his whole body into trying. This was a strength man crumpled under, a power to rip and destroy and massacre and break. Pup could hear the words that came out of him before the jaws clamped down on his head and crushed it like a watermelon. Pup could hear that, in his last moments, Trent did not beg for mercy for himself, nor did he insult his assailants, nor did he cry out for aid from elsewhere. In those moments, Trent asked something of Pup, though knowing he had no right to beseech anything of anyone.

"Help her," he said. "She's not one of them yet."

Pup recognized these words but it did not stop the sharp canines from crunching down and crushing, smashing, disarticulating bits of flesh and bone. The words were said, the teeth descended, and blood and brain and bits began to fly as the strength pressed down and had its way with him, turning his bald head into paste and splinters that slid down Pup's throat with a terrible ease. Pup had bitten down and had completely smashed Trent's head, leaving behind a gushing stump and a body that slid right to the floor, unable to keeps its legs under it. There were words, a request, and while Pup comprehended them, Pup was not doing all of the thinking for Pup.

Houston looked on at this atrocity, and from her arose a deafening scream, which was followed by a feral growl not unlike those of the wolves themselves. Nascent fangs presented, she charged toward Pup, even after seeing such a horrible display, even after seeing that the men from the crew had been thrown like dolls and torn open, slickening the floor with blood and viscera. The hunger and the rage, the wasted blood, the undone meat, the lives lain out spurred her on, and it didn't matter how much raw physical strength and natural acumen for violence she had witnessed, this was a deep-down thing that would play out because it had to and would kill because there was nothing more than to kill, nothing higher.

In the back of Lex's mind, he recognized this beast coming at him, flailing wildly. In the back of Lex's mind, he heard and understood the plea of Daddy's dying right-hand man not far away from them. In the back of Lex's mind were the words of a person seeking the ear of a person to make decisions that people made under such duress. But this was in the back of Lex's mind. In the forefront was the howl of agony, the growl of rage, and a great red pall of hunger cast over all the world before him. The man would have hesitated, but Lex was wolf, and the wolf wanted to shred and rend and tear everything before him. He lunged at the confused, blood-soaked creature before him, the tiny human voice drowned out by the impossible howl at the full moon outside.

She was possessed of a strength and ferocity that exceeded that of a human, her teeth were starting to grow sharp, her muscles starting to possess an unworldly vigor. She was starting to be something that she was not before, and while she could not go back to what she was, nor would she be granted the chance to advance to that which she would be. Soaked in blood already, a single long slice of Lex's powerful claw sprayed out much blood of her own, and while she kept swinging and biting through that pain, she could not make purchase in the muscled and hairy hide of her former friend. He had no such difficulties. She was stronger and fiercer than any person for certain, better than people for certain, but Houston wasn't better than the claws and jaws of the beast that Lex was now.

Lex intercepted her incoming arm and popped it clean out of its socket, reaching over and doing the same with the other one. The shock and the violence turned the belligerent, feral, hissing face of a monster to the awestruck and horrified face of a fragile and mortal and broken young woman now faced with the certainty of a death that she had been just moments from eluding forever. The huge mouth opened, drooling for this promising and blood-soaked mass of flesh, and did not hesitate to shut over the head of one that Lex had once loved, grinding it up into hamburger.

At the back of Lex's mind, Lex wept for her, ill-used and dead, wanting only to be one of those avatars of feminine perfection that Daddy kept. At the back of Lex's mind, Lex softly asked for no more death and no more loss and that it be over soon. Lex remembered, back there, the times in each other's arms, the comfort they derived, could even see the excitement of the moments entertaining Daddy's crew and Daddy's guests by Houston's side sometimes. Lex sat in those memories, inhabiting them and trying to clutch them close but knew that none of that concerned the wolf. The beast in Lex had devoured her as soon as look at her, and that would linger there forever. He expected nothing from this monster that had taken him over; he expected only shouting through a forest of indefinable distance between man and wolf.

Lex anticipated this, the taste of Houston still in that lupine maw, and yet the Lex behind the wolf heard something unexpected, something that resounded throughout whatever this strange prison was; Lex heard the sound of mournful howls escaping not just his lips but those of the others.

FATHERS AND MOTHERS

Blood, rot, roses, drugs, and fine wine. The door was just a door with a doorknob like any other, incapable of stopping a hungry and angry wolfpack. The Pup inside the beast cringed at the thought of what clearly lay ahead. There was a promise that more innocents were about to die but also that those innocents were fast and savage and inveterate bloodletters. They would come quickly and fight hard and tirelessly, and if anyone survived, it would be miraculous. The Pup inside would have expressed this to the wolf bounding onward, pressing muscled shoulders against the door, but there was a distinct possibility that the wolf knew it, that what lay ahead carried this stink for a reason. Even if the wolf didn't, it was hard to call out to the wolf from a place of bodiless contemplation.

The room was full of thick shadows and a long black carpet stained unceremoniously with blood, cum, squirt. It had seemed before to be a void, but it was instead a place suspended in night, a chamber where some were disposed of and some had been indoctrinated with promise of deepest and darkest pleasure. This place was familiar. The air here was thick with visceral memory but with the taint of first mistake. Were there hands all around Pup, stroking the thick, bristly fur from nowhere? Breath of air in perked up ears, the corpse-stink coming close, then backing away, fading, then returning.

"They are ungrateful," said every patch of darkness and every spot of blood on the long black carpet; they spoke in Daddy's voice. "They are ungrateful, and they have come to strike me down and eat my heart."

Moans, cries, hisses, growls. The smell of corpse and rose and blood, faint traces of old perfumes, waft of hashish and opium—the brides were there in this dark waiting, as they had always stayed there in the dark waiting. A trickle of laughter, a sudden sharp pain in Pup's side, a momentary flash of the pale face of the redheaded bride. Pup swung back and found air, then more pain from a gash in their back. More laughter trickling down like tiny raindrops, like the beads of blood. Sighs followed as the figures moving through the void struck more, taking more out of Pup's body, then moving on to the others. It took time, but Pup finally smelled one as she opened her mouth to bite.

The beautiful ladyboy's eyes widened in shock when Pup shoved a clawed hand into her mouth, grabbing hold of a tongue that had brought much pleasure, then yanking it out of her face completely, tossing it to the floor and stomping on it as it writhed about, somehow still alive on its own. With the other clawed hand, Pup dug into her face through the cheek, forcing a mutely inarticulate scream before clawing again and again, shredding into the toned concubine body, until a wide gash opened on her breast. It was a quick, dispassionate stroke that silenced the beating of that undead heart. Still, two more remained.

The redhead came at Lex with a strength matching

the wolfman's own and a tenacity and speed that outshone it. The blonde wound around and joined the attack, even if it meant being open to the others. They should, perhaps, have been protecting the master, who was standing there watching, but were too driven by blood and revenge for their own fallen to think about the preservation of life. Their only concern for life was taking it, and they did their best to do so. The truth was Daddy's protectors were dead and all that was left to rely upon was his own strength and that of the predators he had fed and molded and cultivated. Predation was something they did well; finding an opening and striking came naturally to them.

A gash in Lex's side. A punch to Lex's rippling stomach. A strike from the other flank. The two bore down hard, dodging, weaving, flowing like the blood they spilled and drank and sliding away from strike after strike. Asha kicked the blonde out of the way, claiming space and then coming in to aid Lex from the open right flank, digging claws into the redhead and following up by nonchalantly tearing a big chunk of dead flesh off the vampire bride's body, spitting it out to reveal small squirming tendrils of something mephitic and wormlike, something that didn't look like life but like hardened clots of blood given weird parasitic life. The redhead tried to shake her attacker off, which gave Lex a chance to swing on the other attacker.

Pup hesitated to shove the vampiress away from Asha and take it for their own prey. The human in Pup remembered the awe and passion and even the tinge of love they had experienced for this being, unsatisfied desire to be around her and a sweet memory used to keep them shackled. The human in Pup wanted this woman to escape and see freedom with them, somehow cured of the monstrous state as Houston could not be. But in Pup's head was the sound of howling, the sound of victory, and the smell of fresh blood. The blonde was ready to fight, ready to kill.

With the wolf in charge of Pup's body, there was nothing pulling away, nothing desiring this pale, shining beauty too much to cause her pain. Dead, undead, the pretty blonde head still popped off, a rain of blood and more of the strange, tiny red vermin like giant dinoflagellates swimming in it. The body still flailed out, still clawed and struggled, still twitched, but headless was headless, bloodless was bloodless. The perfect, pallid body of the blonde Pup had once adored and thought on when things were getting unbearably grim hung limp and then finally thudded down, the body no longer able to take blood or writhe in pain or cause harm and therefore of no use to the consciousness inside it, which let the body at last conclude and find more of the rest that had occupied so much of her time in life. Cassilda was dead.

"You would face me, kill me where I stand? Where is your loyalty, Pup?"

Daddy shot forth like a bullet, extending an arm impossibly far and grabbing hold of the massive white wolf that Luna had become and effortlessly lifting her by the throat. It was exactly the vulgar display of power it was intended to be, and even in the world of howls and hunger and hunt, it still resounded in Pup, touched the human part, and suggested that the wolf couldn't save it. Luna wrestled in that grasp, swiping hard but never seeming to connect, even with the growing shape that had caught hold of her.

"I am a king among beasts, stupid animals. I command the likes of you and you dare to leave me brideless, to cut down my allies, and to rebel against me? The wolf bitch is hurt. I can smell it; I can taste it."

The towering creature, all torso, tottered and wobbled and barely held itself aloft on inhuman and impossible legs. It unhinged its jaw serpentwise, a chasm of toothy protrusions between top lip and bottom lip. As Luna struggled, the creature had no trouble getting hold of her furred and strong neck and biting down through mounds of fur and muscle until her artery sprayed. The floor faded beneath Pup and Luna as the blood gushed out unceremoniously into the mouth of their giant and deformed captor, who savored and swallowed it. They descended into darkness as Daddy drank and Luna struggled from lack of blood. Pup's claws held firm, but the body they tried to bite at seemed to squirm and turn perfectly to avoid the incoming bite. Daddy's bite had struck true, and Luna, though she clung tight, was going to die.

In the dark, there was a gleam of red, a pool of red beneath them, an almost unbearable stench of rot and blood and malignant life churning below and waiting for more to contribute to it. Dark, thick tendrils of something were rising and descending from that macabre pool. The wolf nose cut through all possible subterfuge, the wolf nose told them true, and it said, perfectly assured and without any mistake or reservation, that down there beneath them was a writhing, oozing, living pool of blood. Though she took some flesh off as he did, Daddy pulled Luna from him and began to let the gushing lifeforce from her wound spray and drip down into the pool, another life among what must have been thousands.

If Pup could cry out, Pup would have said, "All right, I'll go back." If Pup could cry out, Pup would have begged to stop, said, "No, you bastard, stop!" Pup would have said or done or agreed to absolutely anything to cut short this horrid scene they were stuck in the middle of. Houston had already been claimed, and now, now there were three and the three were facing the power of something old and dark and insurmountable, a living plague that had thrived and gestated and mutated to accommodate even more teeming life.

Was Daddy of the pool or from the pool? Had he created it? Pup could not speculate, Pup could not strategize, Pup could only hold on with one clawed hand and strike with the other, finding the wound that Luna had created as Daddy pulled her off, a gash in his side, a portal into rotted green-black ribs, a body teeming with maggots and other tiny parasites, held together by muscle and stretched over and covered with tissue paper flesh. The invitation was clear.

Pup's claws diced through rib meat, shattered mutable antique bone, took the repellent feel of crawling maggots, tiny beetles, worms, and the little red things and endured them trying to crawl and burrow and bite into thick fur. Daddy had taken another of them, and that was what mattered. Daddy was wounded and open, and that was what mattered. The giant body winced as the great rib cage smashed, as ill-gotten blood gushed forth from that mistake, and though they should have been pulled down toward descent into that terrible bleeding pool, instead the vampire was pushing upward, trying to shake Pup free and let the body drop, but deep as Daddy had gotten into Pup, Pup was now getting into Daddy.

Sinew and nerve, bone and skin and organ meat, Pup dug through and ripped into the body beneath the sumptuous suit, the badge of office. Office or none, Daddy or none, king or none, the flesh was papery, the spirit was waning, and the mighty monstrosity was showing itself no more than a bladder of stolen life and potential reclaimed for no purpose beyond extending and empowering itself, thriving and surviving to the benefit of no one. Pup was strong, Pup was loyal, Pup was beast, and beast was more than a match for vermin, true strength aligned against parasitic greed. Slick with blood and bile, struggling to stay on, Pup followed the trail Luna dug and took out what was needed.

Daddy shook again hard, and Pup, for a moment, lost hold of the wound, starting to tumble but instead grabbing hold of Daddy's other leg and then digging claws into the other side of the body. Broken ribcage and rotting flesh and eldritch insects were streaming out of the wound on the left, but the right side of the body still had more to take. Even if it could not die, even if the meat was rancid, it would still claim this victory over life. Pup clung to the leg and reached up to rend and tear, gaining a stronger hold on this elongated creepy thing. A gash; and through the gash, a way; and through the way, another spurt of blood and disgusting little vermin.

Flesh again gave way. Ribcage, flimsy, made to protect an organ that had done good for no one and had remained unstaked through cagey action, dark promises, and the suite of powers that elevated this grotesquerie near god. Pustulant green rib ripped open, and though there were many potent and dreadful smells, the clearest one to the attuned lupine nose was that of meat and trickle of iron, that of life, and though it was small and rotten, poor quarry for a wooden stake, Pup raised themself up, opened those long, toothy, feral jaws, and took in this tiny black berry of hate, biting down and squeezing out its meager juice. It tasted bitter, almost rancid, and the corpse-waft was overpowering, but Pup kept it down. Pup swallowed it and the last of the stolen blood it could hold.

In its thrash, it floated, again up through the floor, the middle-aged and unremarkable face shifting into something more gaunt and skeletal as flesh shriveled, flesh shrunk away from it. As meat on bone and muscle no longer had moisture to slicken it, it was sloughing, molting as the body returned Pup to the room full of brides to watch in wide-eyed horror as the three wolves stood triumphant over all of the kidnapped and cultivated and brainwashed brides they fought. It watched as the last hopes faded from it, as the body told itself that the source of its lifeforce was now in the guts of its once faithful dog. There was bone and there was rot and there was wound where life had been, and in the end, at the merciful end, there in that chamber, the body, artificially preserved, lost all the things that had preserved it and was left with splintered bone and rotten meat and then, at last, dusty death.

Covered in blood and fluids, barely sentient, still, the pack of wolves saw Pup ascend alone and could tell that while Pup had won over the one that had once been master, Luna was gone, her scent faint and nearly untraceable somewhere below in that bleeding pool of parasites. They were covered in blood and flesh and meat, and yet clearest in their beast brains was the loss of one of theirs, and again, the pack spoke out with a single voice, letting out another long howl of lamentation. Even in this state, they could tell that once more, someone they loved was gone. Even in this state, they came together and held each other, licking strange ichor that stained and marred their fur and feeling the warmth and love that they were developing.

They took little time to rest, though, traveling down a somehow shorter hallway in a somehow smaller building, tethered now to reality as they had known it and then running until they emerged in cool night air under the glow of the moon that had given them the power to survive. They ran, guided away from the streets, away from the lights, away from unnatural scrutiny, and away from the scent of the workings of man, until they nearly collapsed together somewhere else entirely.

HOWL FOR THE LOST

By day, they would have recognized this as a trail deep in Forest Park but instead could think only that it was safe. They were safe to rest but also safe to grieve, still as human as they were wolves. There were things carried from the world of tortured and kidnapped humanity that stayed with them as mighty hounds of the hunt. Towering, powerful Lex sat, elongated legs folded, head down between them. Sleek, wise killer Asha was on all fours, looking up at the moon and letting out a howl for Luna, a howl for Houston, a howl for life as they had known it.

Instinct took over in Pup. Pup approached Asha, stroking the warm fur of their quadruped packmate, reaching down to squeeze small, perky furred tits firmly but affectionately, feeling a stir in a cock that had so often been caged or left soft, feeling the barriers between masc and femme, person and wolf, self and pack dissolve. This was nature and nature did not have to hold back or to judge. The beast that was surging in Pup was what mattered, not notions of who Pup was by day or by night.

Pup smelled a wetness building in Asha, a primal eagerness and a deep connection. Pup's hard-on, scaled for the body of the wolf, throbbed with need and took over judgement. Asha pushed back and welcomed Pup into her, releasing, then squeezing tight, her cunt holding on to something she could not let go of, bond and act alike. The push, the pull, the entwine, the thrum and the hum and the shake, pounding, uniting. The two shuddered with it, the vigorous animal fuck. Pup clamped their sharp teeth down onto her and tightly asserted that they would no more let go than Asha. No one was letting go, not now.

Behind them, Pup felt strong arms take hold of them, felt sharp teeth grazing their shoulder blade. Lex had risen, smelling passion and power and need and gravitating toward this oneness, this wolfness, this ritual of loss and reconnection. Lex had risen in eagerness, what was once clit now turned cock transcending further the bounds that he had once lived with. Lex was ready and rigid and eager to slide into Pup, who did not resist or feel any need to make a display of dominance. Pup backed into the offered cock, and Lex thrust forward into the welcoming hole. They were three, and they were one.

Pup carried on fucking Asha with the same intensity they had as they'd ripped Daddy to shreds to let them out. This was as much an escape and as a time to show the resilience and the power of wolf-flesh. Impossible strength, impossible speed, impossible rhythm wrought of perfect smell and the sharp ears of a dog. Pup could hear heartbeat, smell building fluids, smell sweat pouring from the feral tongue, feel more acutely than ever every motion that was made.

Higher, stronger, faster, better, enhanced—perfected perhaps. Pup rolled Lex over, suddenly overpowering the wolf that had been pounding them. Pup spread

Lex's legs and entered them with a powerful thrust and a shake and a writhe and a shiver of strength, then pounding, eager pounding, thirsty pounding, deep and sweet and nurturing. Asha hovered over Lex's long, powerful tongue, which entered and explored her even as they were being entered. The conduit renewed, they pleasured each other, tempering and forging the connection.

Pack gathered strength from pack; Pack gathered lust and thirst for life from pack. They had shifted positions, and now they shifted again. Pup on Asha, Lex on Pup, then Pup lying down and spreading and being taken by Lex, grinding eager, dancing true. New shapes with each other's bodies, new textures for hands and tongues. Flexible muscles and bones gifted bends at new angles, spines arced further, legs spread far apart. The supple, perfected shape that Asha formed was a thing of beauty, made all the more beautiful because it could be shared, because Asha could be had and Pack could please Pack.

Pack carved marks with razored claws and let blood run cleaner. Pack nuzzled and rolled and wrestles and built again the tension wrought from trauma, and Pack let out confusion and the spilling of too much blood. Pack howled in the night, fleeing at the smell of humans, into other dark spaces, spots where they went and listened, and when it was good and quiet, they took that tension, the fear of being found, and they carried on again, the Three as One.

Marked with scars, marked with pain within and without, they carried on and wrought deep, real animal communion amongst themselves. Bodies bent in passion, bodies moved by power. Tastes of every spot of fur and orifice. Tastes of depths within and without. They fucked until aching like the beasts they were, and they fucked until nearly morning. They could only talk amongst themselves with the passions that they shared and with the might coursing through the wolfish bodies.

They had howled; they had run. They had fucked, and they had just killed. They had shared the worst of their lives, and even still, they were sharing something harsh, but they were sharing something they had never known before. They were sharing not just the communion between bodies but the potential of a free and open world where they had the strength to defend those they called theirs. It was beyond family, it was beyond community, it was the raw, lawless moonlit promise of shared survival.

WOLF AND DOG

Pup was somewhere else even as they fucked and fought and grieved alongside the rest of their pack. Pup was in a strange forest like the last time they had run alongside Millie. As before, Millie was there. There was fur on Millie. There was light in Millie's eyes. There was dog in Millie; there was all the dog there could be. Pup could no longer regard her as NotMillie.

"It was you," said Pup. "It was always you, and it was really you."

"Yes," said Millie, "there is a pack running with you, and they have run for a great long time. You were never alone in all this, but you run at the front of your pack now."

Pup had not even been Master of Pup. Pup had hoped and prayed to be kept and cherished; Pup had relied on others to be Master. Their eyes always seemed so clear, their posture so confident, their minds so sharp and so attuned to what needed to come next. Pup was nothing like that. Pup had lived through Lenore's gift, but Pup didn't feel much like running at the front.

"I'll get them killed," said Pup. "I make bad choices."

"Lenore's ears and nose were sharp," said Millie, "and now she gave you that. Your nose is sharp enough."

"But what do I do?"

"If you must kill to get cash, then kill. If you must kill to get clothes, then kill. If you must kill to eat, then kill. You've joined a hunt; it does not stop chasing."

"That's that? A hunt, a chase, for the rest of life and maybe after?"

"We are a pack of wolves," said Millie.

Who is Garrett Cook

Garrett Cook is a queer, mentally ill author living in Portland, OR with his partner of 8 years. His book Time Pimp is a winner of the Wonderland Award, and his book Charcoal was nominated for both the Wonderland and Splatterpunk awards. He teaches online writing workshops that have led to many students getting work published.

More Books from
Madness Heart Press

The Madness Heart Press Employee Manual

Devour the Eath - A Kaiju Anthology

PLAYS/Hauntologies by Ben Arzate

Exotic Meats & Inedible Objects by Rachel Rodman

The Revised Anarchist's Kosher Cookbook by Maxwell Bauman

Giant Robots of Babel by Maxwell Bauman

Inappropriate Toasts for All Occasions by Michael Allen Rose

The Reattachment by Douglas Ford

Little Lugosi by Douglas Ford

Mania by Lucas Mangum

Gush by Gina Ranalli

Porcelain by Nate Southard

www.ingramcontent.com/pod-product-compliance
Lightning Source LLC
Chambersburg PA
CBHW030903200726
48289CB00003B/877